DISSIDENT

A Story of Conscience in
Cold War Czechoslovakia

BY RODERICK MCDONALD

Printed in the United States of America
ISBN: 979-8-234-03057-3

Cover design by Lindsey McDonald
Interior design by Lindsey McDonald
First Edition

DISCLAIMER

This is a work of fiction. Names, characters, places, and incidents
are the product of the author's imagination. While the Zetor Tractor
Factory in Brno is a real enterprise, the events and characters depicted
in this story are entirely fictional. Any resemblance to actual persons,
living or dead, or to real events is purely coincidental.

For Jane McDonald
With love and admiration

The robber baron's cruelty may sometimes sleep,
his cupidity may at some point be satiated;
but those who torment us for our own good
will torment us without end
for they do so with the approval of their own conscience.

— C.S. Lewis, God in the Dock: Essays on Theology and Ethics

The line separating good and evil passes
not through states,
nor between classes,
nor between political parties either –
but right through every human heart –
and through all human hearts.

— Solzhenitsyn, Aleksandr. The Gulag Archipelago

KOLENCE

LATE FALL, 1971

The morning sun began to glow on the tree-lined horizon as Yuri moved with stealth. The wind stung his face. Layers of wool shielded his body from its bite. He bristled at the thought that a needle or spool of thread could not be purchased, so the holes in his woolen sweater went unmended. Barns, stacked with hay from fall's harvest, were barely visible in the pre-dawn light. The sweet, earthy scent of hay mingled with wood smoke and manure. Wood for cooking was still cheaper and more accessible than coal. He dodged rough patches of the side road, quieting the complaining fenders of his cargo trike to avoid unwanted attention. The drab, colorless *kolchozní byty,* collective farm housing, loomed unnaturally behind him, while the winter beauty of the countryside stretched out before him. He left the collective farm, leaving the Třeboň Basin behind, passing fish ponds and wetlands, and entering stretches of forested land and fields. His fear of being seen leaving the collective eased. Thor, his beloved dog, rushed at his heels, eager to begin a rare adventure. Yuri watched his dog running, tongue hanging to one side, and his heart became heavy, nearly breaking. He put out of his mind what he had to do with Thor.

Before the gray dawn broke, Yuri stole away from the farm without permission, wishing to be seen by no one. Strapped to the trike's platform were two dozen eggs, carefully protected, along with jars of produce and jam that his sister Petra had given him for Father Kaleda—also without permission.

They slowly journeyed to the small village of Kolence. He knew he would pass the graveyard where his mother lay, and was unsure whether he would stop. He chose to postpone the decision.

From an early age, anything mechanical fascinated Yuri— tractors, hay balers, bicycles. It thrilled him to find a castaway bicycle in disrepair, with weeds threading through the frame, the pedals reduced to stubs, and the chain rusted and detached. He would coast around the farm on flat tires, grinning as he propelled himself with his feet, dreaming of how to restore its faded glory.

Over the years, the community recognized Yuri's mechanical skills and rewarded him with work in the collective workshop alongside his father and the other mechanics. Bicycles were a common form of transportation on the collective farm, more accessible than motorized vehicles. Wanting to improve on the bicycle's utility, Yuri fabricated a cargo trike from the remnants of three retired bicycles and scrap metal. With two tires in front, he welded a platform for transporting small loads of grain, vegetables, or repair equipment to other farmers. He was praised quietly for his ingenuity.

Yuri's resourcefulness met the needs of others, sparing them the frustration of waiting for unreliable delivery vehicles. His efforts endeared him to the farmers, but his impulsiveness taxed the patience of the collective decision-makers. It didn't help that these party members frequently overheard rumors of praise directed towards Yuri. Farmers would remark, "Yuri certainly has the Collective Spirit."

However, the party officials overseeing farm operations—the *straníci*—viewed matters differently. Tasked with maintaining ideological discipline, they saw acts of kindness as potential threats to the delicate order they claimed to uphold. After hearing these rumors, their interpretation of Yuri's so-called Collective Spirit began to resemble an Independent Spirit. They saw his three-wheeled creation not as a triumph of ingenuity but as a deviation from standard procedures and a threat to the established order.

Yuri rode past moldering remnants of old land boundaries, nearly erased by time: tree lines and hedge rows, crumbling stone walls, and the foundations of long-abandoned buildings. He recalled his father's stories of their forced removal from the family farm in Kolence. Not a single crown was given in compensation when their land was seized—fields, livestock, machinery—all taken by the state, leaving them with nothing but memories of a life stripped away. He managed to block out the painful memories of his family's forced relocation. He dared not show signs of discontent.

Yuri struggled on the gentle uphill climbs, his legs burning with the effort. But on the long downhill stretches, he would call to Thor, "Hop up, old boy, it's a long way. There's room for you." Thor pressed himself onto the trike's platform, squeezed between the produce and jars, eyes and nose active, working. One moment, he panted clouds of mist; the next, his mouth clamped shut, his nostrils flared, alert to the scent of some unseen creature daring him to give chase. Thor's active nose sequenced and cataloged the scents of pastures and forests as they glided along. Occasionally, he raised his head in recognition of familiar and nostalgic scents or at the sight of a squirrel. Kolence was once his home, too.

It was All Saints' Day, a time when most farmers took their rest. Like rabbits in their warrens, they avoided the scrutiny of the *straníci* by not participating in this cultural tradition. Yuri, however, used this day as cover from suspicious eyes to visit an old acquaintance.

His mind wandered from his dangerous task. He traveled to the home of Father Kaleda, sometimes referred to as "The Blind Priest." Years ago, Yuri attended the Hussite church led by Father Kaleda with his mother and sisters. He was a friend of the family.

Yuri recalled standing beside his father and sisters, gazing at the lonely, silent wooden casket resting six feet under the earth. She was gone forever at a time when he most needed his mother. Father Kaleda had sung a traditional Hussite hymn of lament in his rich baritone, his voice heavy with grief, breaking under the weight of her death. As they left the gravesite that day, the unholy sound of shoveled earth striking her casket shattered the comforting echoes of the priest's lament, and a heavy grief settled over Yuri.

He remembered Father Kaleda's words, spoken later on the day he offered his final prayer over Yuri's mother and laid her to rest.

"Yuri, there is something you need to know. Your mother told me these things a few months ago on the day I visited. Her words were halting. Even then, she struggled to breathe. You may recall that she developed a cough in October. Your father and she both thought it was nothing at the time. They assumed she would recover. Of course, you know, she didn't. She became more tired and lost weight. They grew concerned. The farm was behind schedule in winter field preparation. The agriculture commissars urged that cover crops be planted. Your father had a tractor to repair. He was the only one who could fix it. He protested; they demanded. At last, they left for the regional hospital in České Budějovice. It was too late. The TB was too far advanced."

Yuri stopped his trike. Thor turned to look at him with questioning eyes. Painful memories came with fresh intensity as he approached his old home in Kolence and his mother's grave. He never fully grieved her death. But the memories also held a key to a puzzle about his father.

"Easy, old boy, give me a minute," he spoke to Thor, who grew agitated waiting.

He continued to think about Kaleda's final words on that same day:

"She told me that your father blames himself for the fatal illness. She said that the nightmares from the war years were bad enough for him, but this was different, worse. He overworks to quiet his conscience. Someday, he'll do something rash."

Yuri thought, *"He'll do something rash." And the following year, after* her *death, we lost the farm. If he was in danger when* Maminka *died, is he not more so now?*

One difficulty of that day lay in facing his accusing conscience as he prepared mentally to visit Father Kaleda. Years had passed since moving from Kolence to Třeboň. Though the priest often wrote, Yuri had never responded. Letters came less frequently, and now Yuri asked himself, *Why didn't I ever write back?*

This meeting also presented a tug-of-war between his head and heart. On the one hand, Yuri loved Father Kaleda, a bond forged through shared adversity and joyful memories in the underground church. On the other hand, new ideas about the world weighed on his mind, ideas very different from, and even opposed to, the priest's beliefs.

Thor began whining, pointing his snout into the distance. "Squirrel!" Yuri shouted—the noun that, in their shared language, had long since become a verb. Thor exploded in pursuit, launching from the trike platform, his legs running before touching the ground. A squirrel, unaccustomed to the dog's keen nose, abandoned its hiding spot and bounded through the brown leaves and ferns, vanishing and reappearing in its frantic escape to a nearby tree. Yuri listened to the squirrel's imprecations and watched its tail flick with agitation. Bitterness mingled with the pure delight of watching his dog. *I'm going to miss Thor.*

With travel restricted, this clandestine 14-kilometer journey surprised Yuri with its beauty. He rode past fields, some stubbled from the recent harvest, others freshly furrowed for the next planting season. A buck pursued a doe until they disappeared into the trees lining the field. Soon, Yuri entered a forest of oak and maple, their branches touched by the onset of winter.

A stray thought came uninvited: *These trees reaching toward the sky, the deer and small creatures surviving and thriving by nature's provision, caring for their young, this cannot be the product of chance, of atoms randomly colliding.* The thought startled him, presupposing ideas he did not welcome. He distrusted the pull of Beauty and the message Creation whispered. He hurried on his way.

Yuri first saw the ancient church building, long abandoned. He rode on, past the graveyard, head down, then stopped. He looked back, studying the centuries-old building and the beauty of the Gothic architecture. He was unable to fight against the unseen hand drawing him back to the church graveyard.

He approached it, parked his trike, and paused, bracing himself for a wave of long-suppressed emotions. Passing through a low hedge, he scanned the modest headstones and crosses, searching for his mother's burial site. Being a holiday, other villagers trickled in with flowers or votive candles, unconcerned about watchful eyes. At last, he found a simple concrete headstone and a cross among other markers with familiar names.

Concrete. Why concrete?

Nearly six years ago, he stood here. During this time, his conscience nagged at him. *My mother, the one who least deserved the pain I gave her. She was the first to forgive. And still, I treated her like she didn't matter.* Despite Yuri's training to suppress his guilt, he could not erase this memory. This was what he tried to avoid.

Weeds had grown tall, concealing the lower half of his mother's concrete graveside slab. Eager to finish this visitation, Yuri began retracing his steps but stopped abruptly. He returned, pulled up the weeds, and revealed the writing on the slab:

> All we like sheep have gone astray;
> we have turned every one to his own way;
> and the Lord hath laid on him
> the iniquity of us all.
> — Isaiah 53:6

He stared blankly. The words were laden with the fragrance of his mother. She had quoted scripture like this to her children in the home. His father had warned her of the danger from the State, but she would laugh it off. Yuri had never understood the meaning behind those words, nor why they were considered seditious, and, truthfully, he had never really cared. He hastened away, then stopped and looked back. *Maybe later. Maybe never. I don't care.*

Yuri knew that visiting Father Kaleda would test his worldview. Back at the farm, everything revolved around solidarity, collective purpose, and the welfare of the community—a clear, scientific order. The farmers worked like cogs in a machine under the oversight of the party secretary. This all suited Yuri very well. But here, surrounded by the dead, the value of individual souls cried out from the gravestones, each tended by loving survivors. Before crossing Kaleda's threshold, he sensed the whole village was haunted. Longings stirred—the beauty of nature, the guilt of his past, and grief for his dead mother—threatening the certainty of his sound atheism. He couldn't be too cautious.

THE BLIND PRIEST

LATE FALL, 1971

The path to Kaleda's cottage was well-trodden by feet, hidden among the trees, with no signs of traffic from vehicles or wagons. He stood, mastering his anxiety, remembering the one thing he came to do. Parking his trike nearby, Yuri approached the cottage and studied it. Familiar decorative features depicting folk traditions adorned its humble facade. He paused at the door to examine the intricate yet sturdy ironwork of the door hinges. The contrast struck him: the simple craftsmanship here stood in stark opposition to the gray, drab *kolchoz* apartments, utilitarian buildings neglectful of the souls of their inhabitants, built by soulless workers. He took a deep breath and knocked.

"Come in, Yuri!" Kaleda's voice cheerfully rang out as though Yuri had been away for only a few hours, not years.

Yuri wondered apprehensively, almost shocked. *Can the Blind Priest see through doors? That is exactly what used to bother me about him. He's able to "see" things.* He lifted the latch on the sturdy wooden door and pulled it open. He stared at the latch, crafted from cast iron. Even this bore the design of a lion's head with a sunburst backplate. *Who were these people?*

"You never in the past cared about the craftsmanship of my door knocker. You should look more carefully at the door hinges," said Kaleda.

Yuri didn't speak. He shook his head imperceptibly. Inside, the cottage was rustic and simply furnished: clay pots, crockery, and cast-iron cookware in the kitchen; a sturdy wooden table with two chairs, benches stacked at one end of the room; a straw-padded bed covered by a woolen blanket; a wood-burning stove; and a kerosene lamp. The stove warmed the room and filled it with the fragrance of burning hardwood.

The Blind Priest rose from the table, walked toward the door, groped for where he thought Yuri was standing, and found him. He embraced Yuri warmly, dispelling any fears that the priest might resent his years of silence. He appeared more frail now, his hair and beard white and long. Yet he noticed an intensity and tension behind his friendly demeanor.

Kaleda, now around seventy-five, hailed from the region once known as Moravia. He had been conscripted into the Austro-Hungarian Army. Though he fought heroically, the cruelty of warfare and his participation in it broke him. Multiple exposures to mustard gas had partially blinded him. Upon returning home and finding himself unfit for other work, he pursued a theological education, preparing for ministry, at least, that's what it was called; to him, however, it was merely acting in a theater and a sinecure. He viewed the study of doctrine and Scripture as mere tools of a profession; nothing could touch and heal the deeply embedded memories of war. Or so he thought. The words he had studied for so long out of duty slowly penetrated the granite walls of his doubt and despair. They became words he loved.

"How did you even know it was me?" Yuri asked. He had to ask.

"Has it been so long that you've forgotten me?" Kaleda asked, a smile in his voice. "I haven't forgotten you. The Lord, who took my sight, left me with two good ears. I heard the rattle of that curious machine—your bicycle invention. Who else would come with such a sound? And your footfall, a dog beside you. And the way you alone would knock, like you always did in the past. Five years. What a man you've become, judging by the sound of your voice and the size and strength of your frame! This must be Thor, then?"

Thor's wet snout found its way into Kaleda's welcoming hands. "Such a dangerous name, Thor, and yet such a gentle animal."

Thor had been a gift from Father Kaleda after Yuri's mother's death, a consolation for a grieving youth. Searching for words, Yuri responded quietly and emotionally, "He's a good old boy."

The experience of reunification left Yuri speechless. He felt the sting of the reminder that it had been five years.

"You must have left your home early," Kaleda observed. "And let's see, on All Saints' Day." He paused to consider this fact and smiled to himself. "I have a little food; will you break bread with me?" But something about Yuri's presence wasn't yet adding up. Kaleda braced himself.

Yuri felt the tension growing, and his stomach was not welcoming food. "That's very kind of you, but I won't stay long. I just brought a few things from the farm. Petra thought of it."

Yuri stepped out briefly, relieved by the cool air from his mounting tension, and returned with the farm produce from his trike. Kaleda, bending down to read the contents of the crate with his hands, said, "Oh, Petra." And Yuri could see and hear the old man suppressing a wave of emotion. Kaleda's voice was softer and a little broken: "She must be a young woman by now. May the Lord bless her—and you— for bringing it, especially at such a risk. Sometimes I am in need, and sometimes I have plenty. I've learned to be content in every situation. Yet, today, I think the contentment of plenty is preferred. Thank you!"

How does he survive here all by himself, Yuri thought.

They sat down on rustic chairs and engaged in small talk, reminiscing about shared memories of the past, including Yuri's mother's illness and funeral. Kaleda asked about Yuri's sisters and his father. Yuri studied Father Kaleda through the lens of adulthood, seeing him differently now than he had as a boy and youth. The priest held the air of a simple, plainspoken man, yet Yuri knew better. However, as keen as Kaleda's mind was, the years had worn down his physical shell. Yuri also observed that Kaleda would pause between comments, sometimes position his head as though he were engaging another train of thought.

Yuri considered asking about the Bible verse on his mother's gravestone, but decided against it. *Maybe later.*

Both of them knew the conversation was entering a new stage. More was at risk now. How far could Kaleda trust Yuri? And how firmly could Yuri defend his communist beliefs before this theologian?

Kaleda, attempting to break the ice, said, "Do you remember, long ago, before one of our Sunday meetings, you ran up to me with such a serious face and said, 'My *Maminka* made *koláče* for you, but she didn't bring them because she burned them. Now we have to eat the burned *koláče.*'"

Yuri looked down and laughed silently and convulsively. Kaleda wished he could see Yuri's expression. He reached out and grasped Yuri's hand, recognizing the silent laughter; he too burst into laughter, saying, "You wanted sympathy from me because I didn't take your burned *koláče*!" Kaleda laughed like a child, nearly falling off the chair.

Composing himself and with caution, Kaleda made the first move, innocently and strategically testing the young man's heart and putting him on the defensive. With some pathos, he asked, "I wrote to you. Did you receive my letters?"

Ashamed, Yuri looked down and replied, "Yeah, I got them. I should've answered. I didn't."

"I know you had school, the farm . . . and caring for Thor." Kaleda paused, then continued, his tone a little wary but not accusing. "But you answered honestly. That gives me hope your soul hasn't wandered too far. Do you remember how we were in Kolence—always cautious, you know. We kept watch for the secret police and informers. But we were a small flock, sheltered from the outside world. We felt relatively safe."

He leaned in slightly, with more gravity. "But I have friends in larger towns, like Třeboň, where you now live, who've been taken. Arrested. For resisting state control over their churches. Do you know anything about this?"

Having not belonged to an underground church since his mother's death, all this had escaped Yuri. He was becoming more uncomfortable.

He realized that Kaleda was probing whether he himself might be an informer. He made no reply.

Leaning back, Kaleda continued, "You've likely had instruction in communist ideology at school. They are thorough in that regard."

Feeling his face had grown red, Yuri rallied and responded more brashly than he intended, "Yes, all the time."

Unfazed by the defensive tone, Kaleda pressed on, "Well then, with so much training, you've perhaps cast aside any belief in God, yes? Ten years ago, you were hungry to learn, eager. Not many children ever came to me with questions about the Scriptures or my preaching. But you did. But then you changed, though, through the years. Have you found this new teaching compelling?"

He gestured gently. "Let me at least bring you a cup of tea."

Both welcomed the pause, and Kaleda placed a tea kettle on the wood-burning stove. Yuri had time to collect his thoughts and cool his emotions while Kaleda calculated his next move. The two simple wooden chairs were pulled over to a small table, and the tea was poured. Both sat down again.

Yuri began cautiously and with more respect, "I don't know if I've abandoned God, but I have many doubts. Where was God in the Great War when you lost your sight? Where was he when my father came back from the next war, haunted by the dead and the tears of the living? Where was he when my mother died, coughing up blood in her bed? If there's a God behind all this pain, then I want no part of Him."

Yuri breathed to calm himself. "I've learned a lot through communism. At least it explains what's broken and how to fix it. Christianity didn't stop the Nazis. Communism did. And the promise of a better life now means more to me than some distant reward in heaven."

Yuri attempted to sound convincing, but as he continued to speak, he realized his words rang hollow. His face flushed with shame as he understood that his remarks had fallen short of the respect owed to this kind, venerable man. Kaleda only looked at him with listening respect in his blind eyes.

Kaleda sensed Yuri was losing momentum with his argument. Yuri ran out of words. Kaleda seemed more at ease, reassured that Yuri had not become an informer. "Well said! I'm glad you haven't let go of God entirely. But the spirit you speak with now, it's not the one I tried to pass on to you. Still, I see you've become a man who thinks seriously about these things. That gives me hope. Keep thinking.

"But tell me, do you truly believe communism holds all the answers? That's a strong claim for a theory born of a mere man, Mr.

Marx. With all the learning you've done, history, literature, and the rest, are you free to question it? Free to write or speak ideas that don't conform to Party doctrine?"

This comment disquieted Yuri. It was scandalous to ask such a question, but he didn't know why. He checked himself, realizing the question required thought. After a moment, he admitted quietly, "No, we're not free."

"Exactly! And what would happen if you spoke against the doctrine? Not even to defy it, just to question it. What if you said, just once, "I wonder if there is an authority higher than the Party?" What if you asked, in public, whether the doctrine could be wrong?"

Yuri frowned. After considering this, he replied, "It wouldn't go well. Truthfully, my life would be ruined."

Kaleda spoke evenly. "So, you tell me that communism is robust, that it holds the promises for a better world, that all of the complexity of life is now simply explained? Nothing rises above the ideology, not even moral conscience, and especially not the Scriptures."

He let the thought settle before continuing. "Yet at the same time, you admit you're not free to think otherwise. Not freely. Not aloud. All questions are silenced. Is this the world you wish to live in, where you're not even free to think?"

He folded his hands, his tone soft but resolute. "If communism is true—if it can endure honest inquiry, then why can't it be debated? Why not question it in school, or in the public square?"

He looked gently toward Yuri. After receiving no reply, Kaleda shook his head and said playfully, "I should have trusted you from the start."

Kaleda gestured toward the box. "This produce you brought me, the state sets the quotas. The farm reports what's grown, where it goes. The state decides everything. The state must always know." He smiled, amused. "And yet, your sister gathered it together, and you brought it here. To me. Quietly . . . and without permission." His voice was warm with mischief. "Shall I guess? Your visit today. No permit?" A dry chuckle. "You'd better pray I don't turn *you* in."

Yuri smiled reluctantly.

"And what about the confiscation of your family farm?" Kaleda continued. Yuri's countenance darkened with displeasure. This piece of family history rubbing against the power of the State was never resolved in his thinking. It became a forbidden topic of discussion in the home. Kaleda, with his sixth sense, perceived he had pressed his point far enough.

"Perhaps my words were a bit rough," Kaleda said. "It's been four years, and I have never heard from you. Not once. I still need to know whether you're my friend. I'm glad you've come, but I still don't know why you've come."

Yuri, who had respected Father Kaleda as a boy but never regarded him as a friend, was touched and surprised by this comment. He replied softly, "You'll always be my friend." He paused, unable to bring himself to say the next thing. Both sat quietly for a few moments.

Finally, the Blind Priest said, "You want me to take Thor, don't you?"

Yuri knew better than to act surprised, but he felt it. "Yes, I came because of Thor." His voice cracked. "My father's taken a position in Brno, working at Zetor Tractor Factory. We'll be living in a *byt* now. Dogs aren't allowed."

Yuri explained further, describing his father's decision to pursue better wages and provide his children with greater educational opportunities. "It all happened fast. I know my *táta* loves the farm. He loves the quiet, the animals, the machines, especially the machines. I never thought he'd leave it behind, that we'd move to the city. He's a different man since *maminka* died."

After more conversation, Yuri became anxious to leave. They both walked out of the cottage. "Thank you for taking Thor. You can keep the box I brought the produce in. You'll find a food and water bowl for Thor and some food scraps."

Kaleda said, "Thank you, Yuri. *Rád jsem, že mohu pomoci. . . .* Walk in the truth."

Yuri wished to make a swift retreat, but before he got far, Kaleda called out, "Yuri, do you have a few minutes? There's one more thing I wish to speak with you about."

21

REGRET

LATE FALL, 1971

They resumed their seats around the rough-hewn wooden table. The hours of the day marched on, and Yuri grew uneasy. Kaleda hummed the tune of a familiar hymn as he heated water for more tea. Yuri looked at the sweater he was wearing, with the familiar holes in the elbows. He remembered that Kaleda had worn the same sweater five years ago. His warmth and respect had grown toward his former "priest", yet he remained more uneasy than before about what Kaleda might "see."

"Your move to Brno is unusual, no?" Kaleda asked. "You remember, don't you, what I said to you about your *Táta* on the day of your *Maminka's* funeral?"

"Yes, I remember."

"Do you think your move to Brno has anything to do with what I said about him?"

"It crossed my mind earlier today," said Yuri.

"Well, I'm glad you thought of it. There may be more to your move than the need for educational opportunities. How has your father been since she died?"

Yuri said, "Quieter than usual. Withdrawn. He works too much. He works to forget."

"I remember when I spoke to your *Maminka* on that day, she also talked about you. You were getting into more trouble than usual." Kaleda smiled. "Things like opening the gates for the pigs so that they escaped; hiding rabbits in the storage shed."

Yuri laughed his silent, convulsive laugh, but became nervous about the direction of the conversation. People didn't talk about their personal lives on the collective; Kaleda was coming dangerously close.

"Yuri, sometimes when a loved one dies, there can be guilt. It can be a force for good or for evil. I'm afraid it's for evil with your father. How it will end, I don't know. And what about you? Did you become reconciled to your *Maminka* before she died?"

Yuri slowly stood and began pacing. He collected his thoughts. He felt an emotional deadlock. The faculty of speaking about his personal life had grown dormant.

Yuri responded, slightly annoyed, "How do you know whether or not I had become reconciled with my *Maminka* before she died, or whether I had anything to be reconciled about?"

Kaleda answered calmly, swiftly, his voice deeply resonating, "I knew your *Maminka*, probably better than you. And I hear it in your voice."

Yuri sat, resigned. As he began to talk, the effort relieved some long-held emotional pressure. He felt a trembling in his chest as he spoke. "Yes, there is one incident I cannot forget. This happened in fact on the same day you visited years ago. . . ."

Petra and Zofia returned to the kitchen after serving their mother in the bedroom. Yuri slipped in for breakfast, stone-faced. Zofia spoke quietly, earnestly, so as not to trouble their mother. "Why do you punish *Maminka*? Have you greeted her this morning?"

Yuri prepared himself a cup of tea, saying nothing.

"Do you even care that she's *dying*? Father Kaleda's coming today. He's going to pray with her, and they'll be praying about you. How do you like that? He'll know what you've been doing."

Yuri paused his breakfast preparation, looking up at the ceiling as his jaw muscles tightened. He didn't care about what Father Kaleda knew or whether he prayed. He was angry with God for allowing his mother to die. Sitting at the table with a simple breakfast, he turned his chair away from his sisters to avoid their eyes.

Don't say anything else. Just stop.

Zofia prodded more, "We found the evidence on your shoes. We told *Maminka.* She knows you opened the gates for the pigs two nights ago. Farmers . . . chasing pigs for hours. *Táta* came in after midnight. Stupid boy. You could have at least cleaned the you-know-what from your shoes."

Yuri slammed his cup down, causing tea to erupt over the brim, and left for school. Petra stared at her sister, wide-eyed, shocked at Yuri's outburst and unaccustomed to Zofia's bristling tongue. The girls stifled a laugh when he returned to gather the books he had forgotten.

Waiting to ensure her brother was gone, Petra finished Yuri's leftover breakfast. Zofia stared at her brother through the window as he walked to school, unsatisfied by her victory.

In class, Yuri's stomach growled. The morning routine droned on as he tried to focus on mathematics, literature, and science. He knew better than to draw attention to himself by excelling—not that he wanted to—or underperforming, though today, he was perilously close.

Zofia's stinging words replayed in his mind, disrupting his concentration. His thoughts became a courtroom where the voices of his conscience clashed in debate. One voice rose to defend him—a heated argument favoring party ideology over his mother's religion, dismissive of family sentimentality. Hot and angry, it echoed his teachers and the collective decision-makers. But another voice interrupted, calm and contrary, like a prosecuting attorney. It carried the weight of Father Kaleda's years of teaching and his mother's quiet influence. The prosecution and the defense clashed, each asserting its authority in a battle for the conscience.

"Yuri, you're not listening. What's the matter with you—empty head." His teacher's tone was sharp.

Heat crept up the back of Yuri's neck. At that moment, any partiality he held for his teachers diminished fast. He stared at the desk, studying the familiar patterns of the wood grain and the shallow etchings left by other comrades-in-suffering over the years.

He hated her. He hated everyone.

The chair scraped hard against the floor as he shoved it back. It tipped, crashing behind him, drawing attention, but he didn't stop. Without a word, he turned and walked out early, heading for the cafeteria.

Yuri arrived first; a while later, the other students trickled in. He found a seat on a long wooden bench. He glanced across the cafeteria, making sure to avoid Zofia above all. He kept his head down and did not wish to engage with his peers. Those who arrived later dared not sit near him. Silencing the protest of his stomach had become his sole concern. And to be left alone. Zofia entered, took a different aisle, and unintentionally sat near him among friends. The sunlight streaming from large windows partially blinded her from seeing Yuri.

At age 15, Zofia was growing increasingly self-conscious about her appearance. Her friend Alena had the extraordinary privilege of traveling to Vienna each summer to visit her grandparents. During these trips, Alena would smuggle back old issues of *Burda Moden,* a renowned fashion magazine. After dinner, Zofia would slip like a shadow to Alena's house. They would draw the curtains, dim the lights, and devour the forbidden images of Western fashion together.

The magazine featured selected patterns for the latest styles, and Zofia, emboldened, chose one. Unable to obtain the colorful fabric depicted in the pages, she settled for the earth-toned, coarse-woven cotton fabric available at the collective farm. Although she couldn't match the colors, she could replicate the design. Over many weeks, in a corner of the living room, her family heard the snipping of scissors and the rhythmic hum of a sewing machine.

On this day, Zofia wore a dress mimicking the adult fashion one might see in Vienna, full of intricate cuts and details. The young boys were oblivious, but the girls were not. Some girls approved, admired, and said nothing, while others leaned in closer, whispering restlessly. A word, like a barb, reached the ears of one of the boys. He had no plan for what he would say. He intended to make a show of his party loyalty more than to provoke or embarrass a girl.

Vojta spoke to Zofia loudly, ensuring many could hear, "Zofia, did your dress come from America? Maybe you would be happier living there. Perhaps your *Maminka's* sick because you're too busy dressing up and not helping her." He had succeeded in drawing attention. She felt all eyes upon her. Stunned and humiliated, her complexion flushed, the vanity of her dress turning into shame, and her eyes shimmering with unshed tears, Zofia left the cafeteria. But she was not so hasty as to miss what happened next.

Yuri, at 16, was a young man who matured physically faster than most. His strength came from the long hours he spent assisting his father in the mechanics' shop. It was unfortunate for Vojta that Yuri heard his public denunciation of Zofia. Without hesitation, he stood, strode over to Vojta, took his head, and thrust his face into a bowl of goulash. Vojta emerged swinging, soup dripping ignominiously from his face, red with anger and paprika. But he was no match for Yuri. With ease, Yuri hoisted Vojta over his shoulder and carried him through the cafeteria, Vojta's fists flailing from his skinny arms, thudding weakly against Yuri's back. His ambition for recognition did not match his diminutive physique. All conversation ceased. All eyes shifted from Zofia to Yuri. He lugged him past the gaping students, through the door, and pitched him outside.

Zofia's lips came together, forming a slight smile.

Yuri retreated to his father's workshop, helping with tasks while waiting for the consequences. His father glanced at him, eyebrows raised, knowing better than to speak. Despite Yuri's sullen, adrenaline-charged demeanor and decision to skip school, his father was glad to have him by his side. He gave Yuri his sandwich.

". . . I know this hurt my *Maminka*. She always hated it when I fought. I seldom went to her after that because I felt justified in what I had done. I keep thinking about it. We really didn't talk much together after that day."

Yuri sat down, emotionally spent.

Kaleda sadly turned towards Yuri, "I'm sorry to hear all this. I can assure you that your *Maminka*, though hurt by your withdrawal of affection, still loved you until the end. Remember what I said about your father: there's a grief that can lead to destruction. I don't know what that means for him or for you."

There was a pause in the conversation. Both sat quietly, holding their cups of tea, each lost in thought. Finally, Kaleda began, "I sense you're eager to leave. I understand. . . . I've been praying about something for a long time, and I think I now have an answer."

Kaleda went to a shelf, retrieved an envelope, and returned. "The church is small now. Some of my people have faced harassment from local authorities. Others? Left under pressure. Is this a bad thing? In one sense, yes. But in another, well, it's purified the church. I've been given warnings. Verbally, and in writing. Not subtle. The point is, I may be arrested soon. One day, you'll hear that I've been arrested. I can't say how I know, but I do. It's coming."

He reached beside him and held out the envelope. "When that day comes, return here. Bring this with you. Follow the instructions inside. Until then, you must keep it well hidden. You will endanger yourself and your family if the wrong people find it. If you take it, please give me your word you will not open it until the time comes."

Kaleda's words hung in the air. *What makes him think I'm willing to suffer for what he believes?* What a s*trange thing to ask.* Yuri took a sip of tea and finally said, "What?"

Kaleda didn't flinch. He repeated himself just as plainly, as though it were the most natural thing in the world, as though he had no doubts that Yuri was the perfect candidate to entrust with this secret and needed clarification.

Uncomfortably, Yuri received the envelope, held it lightly—not wanting it at all—then secured it in his pocket. Looking into Kaleda's partially blind eyes, he said unconvincingly, "I promise."

Yuri left Kaleda's home with mixed feelings—sad to part with an old friend, yet uneasy at his gift for exposing what he preferred to keep private. He felt for the unwelcome envelope in his breast pocket. Moving swiftly, Yuri pulled out a rope from his pocket and tethered Thor to a tree. Despite Yuri's private words of comfort, Thor was agitated and whined. As Yuri departed, Thor strained at the rope and groaned plaintively. He rode away, and with increasing distance, the sound of Thor's groaning diminished. Passing the cemetery on his return home, Yuri's sorrow overwhelmed him.

BRNO

LATE FALL, 1971

Yuri drifted in and out of sleep after collapsing upon the wooden bench of the train car. The day came when Yuri's family departed for Brno. Yuri, Zofia, Petra, and his father, Václav, dressed nicely for the occasion. They labored to prepare and rushed to the train station in the early morning. Many friends assembled with them and wished them farewell. Among these, the Krčméry family gave the longest hugs. Yuri and his father, Václav, shouldered most of the burden of transporting and loading the family's belongings. At last, he found rest and comfort in the monotony of movement and sound: the gentle, slow sway of the train carriage and the four-beat clatter of wheels passing over the track joints. The train whistle sounded distant inside the train car, like in a dream. He resisted the urge to give in to sleep.

Yuri forced himself to think of Thor, the puzzle of their sudden decision to move to Brno, his conversation with Father Kaleda, the clash of worldviews with him, and the envelope. *Why did he give me this envelope?* He had expected someone old, broken by time and loneliness, with watery eyes, but instead, he found a man young in spirit, able to parry his rigid communist views with a smile and disarming warmth. Speaking with Kaleda was such a singular experience that he found himself returning to their conversation again and again. *"If communism is true for all reality, why can't it be debated?"*

Yuri's mood brightened as he listened to his sisters' lively chatter about the ever-changing scenery revealed by the rising sun. Trees along the tracks occasionally obstructed the view, causing sunlight to flicker across the faces of his sisters. They traveled eastward through the rolling hills of Southern Bohemia, where thick mists blanketed the lowlands. As they curved downhill, it seemed the entire train might be swallowed by the fog. Fields held remnants of summer crops, winter wheat, and barley. In the distance, a small deer could be spotted foraging. As they traveled through towns such as Mikulov, Znojmo, and Vranov nad Dyjí, the sisters pointed out medieval castles, churches, and historical buildings with clock towers. Zofia spoke knowledgeably about each sight.

Thousands of starlings rose from their roosts, animating the skyline and dancing in synchronized waves. Everyone was mesmerized by the sight. Moments later, Yuri noticed a solitary kestrel perched among the skeletal limbs of a maple tree, its silhouette stark against the brightening sky. The contrasting scenes unsettled him, like a mirror into the past—the warmth of community—and a lens into the future—of solitude.

He would miss the farm. His thoughts drifted to an event he had witnessed months earlier. In the communal dining hall at the farm, long wooden tables and benches were arranged, where meals of stew, soup, bread, and potatoes were served to the workers. Seating was open, and one day, a youth of Zofia's age mustered the courage to sit across from her. Yuri knew this boy; he worked hard, breaking and turning over the soil with animal-drawn plows. He had a reputation for his strength and skill in handling farm animals. By day's end, he would be famished. Hungry as he was, sitting across from Zofia and smitten by her beauty, he couldn't eat.

Yuri was aware that Zofia liked this hardworking boy, yet, in her quiet manner, she could do nothing to coax him to speak. *She*, however, could at least eat. With her head lowered, she glanced up at him through long lashes, a shy smile playing on her lips as she asked softly, "You must be hungry, no?" But the burly young man mostly looked down, shoulders hunched, saying nothing. After some time, realizing others had noticed him and his untouched food, he flushed, stood up, and left, abandoning his meal.

Zofia met Yuri's lazy stare, and, embarrassed, he turned away.

"Why are you looking at me?" she insisted. Yuri remained mute.

She resembled her mother in appearance but inherited her father's dark eyes and hair. Tall, slender, and well-formed, she moved with delicacy and poise. "Nature had surely formed her in a partial mood," he once overheard Emilie Krčméry say to a friend, not knowing she was quoting from *Jane Eyre*. In her presence, the boys on the farm were rendered mute and awkward. Speaking to her required boldness beyond their reach. And severe punishment was preferable to her frown.

Her curiosity extended beyond the state-approved books of the collective farm. When she discovered a forbidden book owned by a family friend, she spent hours after work or school manually transcribing it. Day by day, she used the pages of inexpensive propaganda and ideological pamphlets, writing in fine pen between the lines and in the margins. The Krčméry family trusted and welcomed dark-eyed Zofia, who spent her evenings hunched over a desk for hours. With the Dvořák family's departure from Třeboň, it was Zofia who was missed most on the farm.

Despite family protests, Zofia resisted the least. *She's not meant for the farm. City life suits her—nobody knows your name there, and she'll like that. Still, the farm kept her in one place, as a wild horse corralled in a field.*

When thinking about Zofia, you couldn't help but compare her to her sister. Petra took after her father: a practical beauty with her mother's fair skin, bred for hard work, broad-shouldered, energetic, voluble, and strong. Yuri had overheard other young men admiring the muscular definition of her arms. She thrived in the company of other young women during the harvest season, laughing, telling stories, and working together to can, pickle, or dry food—a true daughter of communism. And of all his children, Petra worried Yuri's father the most. The one most celebrated by party members on the farm was also the one who protested the loudest against the move to Brno.

Yuri's attention drifted to his father, Václav. No task seemed beyond his capability. Though his solid build might have appeared unremarkable, his strength surpassed that of other men. His children likened him to a swan, destined never to remarry. Yuri was old enough to notice women seeking his attention, some casting over-the-shoulder glances, while others, more openly, offered food under the pretense, "So your children may have more time for study." Indifferent to their attentions, no woman could rival the deep, near-idolatrous love he had for his late wife.

Yuri could not recall ever hearing his father raise his voice except once. One spring day, while walking together along the edge of a field, Yuri almost stepped on a poisonous adder. "Yuri, watch your step!" his father warned abruptly. Yuri was more startled by his father's voice than the snake in his path.

Václav interrupted Yuri's thoughts and leaned closer to Yuri, keeping his voice low to avoid being overheard by the girls. "That little trip out of the village—you took it a couple of weeks back. You didn't think anybody noticed? No permit. Why'd you do that? We could've gotten one easily. There was no need to risk it."

Stunned, Yuri grasped the severity of his actions. "Who knew?" he asked.

"A friend," Václav replied. "He warned me. He didn't want trouble for the family. Somehow, he knew you didn't have a permit. And if he knew, others did too. You were walking a razor's edge. If it had been someone else—someone loyal to the Party, someone who didn't owe us any favors—this could've ended badly."

He paused, then added, "The boy you gave the trike to—he helped smooth things over. When we move to Brno, life will be different. You won't be able to 'cut corners' with regulations as easily. Do you understand? Without our jobs at Zetor, it gets hard for all of us."

He spoke gently, yet Yuri felt the weight of this understated correction. He hated it when he displeased his father.

Nearly every time they entered a train station, officials from the *Československé státní dráhy* in dark uniforms would march onto the train. Permits were checked, identifications inspected, and each passenger's stated purpose of travel was verified. Their manner was always intimidating. Weary from lack of sleep, his mind drifted from reality, paranoid that he would be discovered and arrested for riding his trike to Kolence, or for the envelope he carried. *Why did he give me this envelope?*

As they entered Brno, the Dvořák family admired the city's many sights, including the 13th-century Špilberk Castle perched atop a hill and the Cathedral of St. Peter and Paul, with its impressive Gothic architecture rising against the skyline.

The train's rhythmic chugging slowed, and the brakes screeched as it arrived at Brno Main Railway Station. The doors opened to the smell of diesel exhaust.

With the help of a porter, they loaded their belongings onto a tram. A short ride from the main depot brought them to the Kotlanova tram stop, where they disembarked, surrounded by all their earthly possessions. As the tram pulled away, the excitement of the past weeks leading up to their journey, the thrill of train travel, and the promise of a grand destination seemed to drain away. The long-awaited moment came and went.

Across a dreary ravine stood their destination: a grey, monotonous, sprawling eight-story apartment complex—a *paneláky*, their new home. Studying it, Petra was reminded of the rabbit hutches back on the farm, and she let everyone know.

Exhausted and hungry, they stood in silence. Reading their thoughts, Václav finally said, "We can't look back. We're almost there."

A group of youths, both boys and girls, were playing *fotbal* in the ravine. They seized this day of sunlight and warmer temperatures for one last game of the season. The curiosity of a family appearing lost arrested their game. A contingent peeled off and approached the Dvořák family.

Sabrina, a handsome brunette with wild hair tousled from the game, led the way. She stood tall, over six feet. She eyed them with suspicion. "Welcome to Brno," she said, her tone suggesting a question as if asking, "Are you sure you're in the right place?"

While making introductions, Sabrina appraised the travelers. Noticing their slower, more deliberate way of speaking and glancing mostly at Yuri, she remarked, "Your accent suggests you're from the Southern Bohemian region."

Josef, one of the athletes, was less skilled at affectation. He threw the ball back to the other players and resigned himself to helping these country rubes. *Pitch-fork people.* Sizing up Yuri with a critical eye, he did not care much for this new rival or how Sabrina looked at him.

Yuri answered, self-conscious of his rural dialect, "We were from the collective farm at Třeboň. My *Táta* and I have come to work at Zetor. My sisters will be studying at a couple of different universities."

Josef's initial thought was dismissive. *So you're farm brutes— strong enough to carry your luggage, so we can return to our game.* But then, noticing Zofia and Petra as if for the first time, his interest in helping improved, and his tongue froze.

After completing their move, saying goodbye to their new friends, and finishing supper, Yuri bundled up and stepped out into the ravine after sunset. He took in the strange sights of concentrated humanity, thankful for this open space as a retreat. The collective sounds of honking horns and the distant hum of machinery contrasted sharply with the peaceful sounds of nature he had left behind. Exhaust fumes and industrial emissions replaced the scents of soil, livestock, and warm manure in the evenings. He scanned the night sky for the constellations Orion and Taurus, but the city lights and smog obscured them. The rising moon wore an orange hue.

His thoughts turned to Sabrina, replaying their brief conversation in his mind. Even she seemed different—more polished, more socially adept, and more refined in her speech compared to the girls on the farm. He regarded her height as striking. He held her in cautious esteem but then decided he didn't want to think about her. *She's probably 'trouble'.* The more he tried, the more he failed.

ZETOR

LATE FALL, 1971

The *paneláky* were only minutes from the Zetor Tractor factory by the tram. Yuri Dvořák disembarked, eyes wide as he took in the vast complex before him. Its size surpassed anything he had imagined, making the mechanics' workshop in Třeboň—once his entire world—seem quaint and primitive by comparison. The hum of machinery, which had dampened his spirits the night before, now held a promise of cheerful expectation.

At the main entrance, an early model red Zetor Z 25 tractor stood displayed, inviting Yuri's fingers to trace an arc around the large rear wheel, up and down the chevron treads. Beside him, as expected, his father appeared unmoved.

Following written instructions, Václav navigated to the human resources department, with Yuri trailing closely behind. He had expected a sterile, impersonal welcome from a pale, hollow-chested staff member. Instead, they were warmly greeted by a man who looked like a factory worker. His dirty overalls were smudged with oil, and his calloused hands bore grease marks and bandages. Without hesitation, the man embraced Václav, catching him completely off guard with his appearance and open greeting.

"Greetings and welcome, Captain. You recognize me, don't you?" he said heartily with a distinct Moravian accent.

"Miloslav—look at that. It's been a long time. I didn't think you'd be the one to greet us, but here you are." Václav's tone remained composed, and his words were chosen with care. Introductions to Yuri were made, and Václav surveyed the room quickly.

Yuri noticed that this greeting affected his father, whose usual self-control momentarily slipped. His father's shoulders stiffened under the embrace, and the muscles around his eyes tightened. Yuri turned his attention to Miloslav—a ruddy, barrel-chested man with a somewhat round face and an unexpected fire in his eyes. *There's something more about this man than what I'd expect from a factory worker.* Then came a startling realization: *Captain? He said, Captain. Táta never told me he was a captain in the Soviet Army. He told me almost nothing . . . and I never asked.*

The conversation between Miloslav and his father was urgent; words overlapped, sentences were trimmed. Yuri pieced together fragments: Miloslav had once served under his father's command. They spoke of the Battle of Sokolovo in eastern Slovakia, the liberation of Czechoslovakia from the hated Nazis, and the fates of unaccounted-for comrades, whether dead or alive.

Yuri had never envisioned his father as a leader of men, but the deference and respect Miloslav showed him revealed qualities Yuri had overlooked. He began to understand how his father's steady, calm demeanor—so familiar in the face of the unreasonable demands from the *předseda* at the mechanics' workshop in Třeboň—must have been an invaluable asset amid the chaos of war. Yuri now pictured his father shouldering the weight of battlefield decisions with a steady hand.

They excused themselves and stepped aside to speak privately, an exchange that struck Yuri as unusual and unexpected. Miloslav's eyes darted around the room, scanning for anyone who might be watching too closely. A man who appeared to be a seasoned employee walked toward them. Miloslav abruptly ended the meeting, parting with a smile for both Václav and Yuri.

The orientation conductor approached stiffly, greeting Yuri and Václav while expressing mild surprise at Miloslav's presence away from his workstation. Yuri glanced at his father in disbelief at how he maintained an air of impassive calm. Miloslav, too, eluded suspicion with his friendly, reckless demeanor before slipping away. It was as though they conspired together to toy with the orientation conductor. Yuri and Václav joined a larger group for the factory orientation.

Over the next few days, they were introduced to the factory's culture and values, safety protocols, and the integration of party ideology into every facet of work. Emblematic of this training, prominently displayed on the factory floor and in the break room, was an image of Gustáv Husák, the General Secretary of the Communist Party of Czechoslovakia. For the more energetic workers, there were endless evening courses on diverse subjects. The ravenous, far-reaching Party bureaucracy recruited from the working-class; the ambitious would sacrifice evenings for the hope of career advancement and material privileges of a party bureaucrat. But Yuri was not interested.

They had entered a new world of communist indoctrination; it had been taken to the next level. The consequences of deviation would mark you as an enemy of socialism, followed by the usual threats. Warnings against strikes were especially delivered with cold precision. The argumentation against strikes seemed convincing: if the means of production belonged to the worker, then striking against the factory was, in fact, to strike against themselves. But the warnings were calculated to frighten. *Why would anyone strike? Why are these warnings so severe?* Yuri thought. He looked at his father, who, as usual, was stone-faced.

Eventually, Yuri was assigned to an assembly line station where workers installed the electrical components of the tractor. He impressed his mentor by quickly mastering the installation of batteries, wiring harnesses, switches, gauges, and lights. The mentor recognized his potential and recommended him for rotational assignments at different assembly line stations. Others also noticed.

Over the next three months, Yuri gained experience in frame and chassis assembly, engine installation, transmission and drivetrain, hydraulic systems, and cab and operator controls. He approached the work as though it were a game created solely for his enjoyment. Yuri's performance at work didn't go unnoticed. Rumors circulated that the press would soon arrive to photograph and feature him in a story, casting him as a kind of Communist celebrity. Yuri, too naive to anticipate trouble, failed to understand that some resented the attention he received.

After resuming his role on the electrical parts assembly line following his rotations, one day, Yuri received a written reprimand from his immediate supervisor, who promptly left without a word.

> . . . I am writing to address a matter of significant concern regarding the quality of your work at Zetor, specifically in relation to recent performance evaluations and feedback from our quality control team. It has come to our attention that your work has failed to meet the expected standards, adversely affecting production efficiency, product quality, and customer satisfaction. As a valued member of our team, it is essential that you uphold the highest standards of quality and craftsmanship in your work in accordance with Zetor's commitment to excellence.

He read the letter. He read it again, his expression remaining blank for a moment, then carelessly stuffed it into his pocket, looked around, and resumed his tasks. After a moment, he glanced around again to check if anyone witnessed the exchange. He felt a burning sensation in his chest. He anticipated celebrity, but was humiliated instead. He meticulously reviewed each step of his actions in his mind as he worked, taking a mental inventory of every detail. He repeated this process again and again until he was convinced that the problem did not originate with him.

INTROSPECTION

LATE FALL, 1971

That evening, in their small apartment, Petra chopped garlic while preparing the *večeře*. Yuri sat at the table, staring out at the quiet ravine and the fading afterglow of the setting sun. Petra noticed his brooding silence. As she cut garlic for the *česnečka*, she playfully tossed a piece at Yuri.

He felt it hit his head, watched it bounce onto the linoleum, glanced at Petra, clearly pleased with herself for this provocation and her dead aim. Yuri responded with a furrowed brow, but the slightest smile in his eye, "Stop wasting garlic."

Petra, undeterred, paused briefly before speaking again. "Zofia and I were almost hit by falling plaster today at Market Square."

Yuri glanced away from the ravine, reluctant to be drawn into conversation. "I'm sorry to hear that. You need to be careful. I just got hit by a piece of flying garlic." But the image of buildings falling into ruin stayed with him.

Petra said, "Yuri, you're quieter than usual tonight."

Forcing a smile, he replied, "Yes, that's right."

Respectfully, she held her tongue. Václav, tipped off by Petra's comment, looked up from his newspaper, his eyes peering over the top without turning his head.

Mealtime discussions were typically cheerful, characterized by the vivacious chatter of Petra and Zofia. That night, in rare form, they talked about the new foods they had tried in the city and the latest fashion trends. They playfully gossiped about city girls, mimicking their speech and describing their hairstyles. Václav and Yuri exchanged glances, shaking their heads and laughing with their eyes, pretending to find the conversation childish while secretly enjoying it.

Zofia, exhibiting a flair for mimicry, imitated the local's speech in a softer, slower, and more lyrical manner, using a regional vocabulary. Everyone erupted in laughter. Yuri had been briefly cured of his melancholy. Zofia looked at Yuri, pleased with his transformation.

The conversation ran aground, however, when the topic turned to makeup. Yuri interrupted, "Petra, have you and Zofia felt safe taking the early morning trams to school?"

Petra assured him they had, exchanging a knowing smile with a more sober Zofia, who turned away and straightened her back, pretending to disregard Yuri's concern. Zofia, who could bend others to her will with a glance or the tilt of her head, was most vulnerable when she had something to hide.

Yuri read what Zofia tried to conceal and said, "So there's something more to your trips than admiring beehive hairstyles?"

Both girls fell silent, and Petra cautiously glanced at her sister.

Zofia shrugged in a way that seemed to say, innocently, "Not really." Then she turned to Yuri, her head bowed slightly, her eyes speaking: "Don't you dare ask me another question."

Silence ensued, and Yuri passed the interrogation to his father with a glance. Václav, now interested and somewhat concerned, laid down his paper and said, "Tell me."

Zofia hesitated but couldn't resist the force of her father's simple command. She normally spoke with a velvety contralto voice, but the stress of her admission strained it. Reluctantly, she admitted, "There's a young man on the tram. He started speaking to me. He said his name is Sergei. That's all. It's nothing." Petra raised her eyebrows as though asking, "It's nothing?"

Zofia folded her arms decisively and looked away. She picked up a glass as though to drink, but it was empty, and she set it down.

Václav studied his daughter, reading the defiance in her expression. He rubbed his forehead. "On the outside, people look one way. But on the inside? It's not the same, often," he said, his eyes filled with sadness as he gazed at his beautiful daughter. To Zofia, the fewer the words her father spoke, the heavier she felt their weight.

Yuri's thoughts rose unbidden as he lay on his bed, staring at the ceiling. Refusing to be crushed by his troubles, he resolved to prove that the blame for the malfunctioning tractors would not be pinned on him. His rotations across assembly line stations gave him more than fragmented knowledge; they offered him a holistic understanding of the tractor and the work crews. He mentally rehearsed a strategy for resolving the problem: *Faulty assembly? Defective components? A false negative during testing? What did I observe from the work habits of others at the different stations?*

In his mind, he drew a line from the problem—the control panel—through all the systems that depended on it. Methodically, he began eliminating the impossible, narrowing his focus to the most likely causes. Forming a mental list of hypotheses for further testing, he paused to confront another challenge: *How will I test this?*

Having resolved *how* to address the problem, he dared to ask himself the harder question: *Why did this happen? I know what Kaleda would say: "I think you have a problem with your Communist doctrine fitting into the real world." My response to him: "We'll see about that. If my diagnosis is correct, everything will be cleared up tomorrow— they'll admit their mistake, proving you wrong."*

Sleep did not come easily.

JUDGMENT

LATE FALL, 1971

The next day, while his coworkers broke for lunch at Zetor Tractors, Yuri seized the opportunity to investigate the problem of the broken tractor without authorization. He walked briskly, looking over his shoulder, to the quality control station, where a few tractors bore tags listing problems attributed to him. He confirmed the problem by attempting to start one.

Yuri followed the plan he had devised the night before. He conducted a visual inspection, tested the buttons and switches, and then removed the control panel to examine its wiring, connectors, and circuitry. Using a multimeter, he tested voltage, resistance, and continuity at key points in the system. It didn't take long to identify the fault, correct it, and reinstall the panel. He repeated the process for one more tractor, all within the lunch break. Curiously, it was the same problem.

To test his work, he started each tractor, listening to the cylinders detonate and ensuring all the functions on the control panel operated flawlessly. Satisfied, Yuri gathered his courage, clutched the crumpled reprimand in his hand, and sought out his supervisor. Flattening it out and handing it to him, he confidently explained why it had been issued in error and how he resolved the problem. Together, they went back to both tractors, where Yuri demonstrated their perfect operation.

Meanwhile, returning from lunch, the quality control team lingered nearby, their eyes on Yuri with veiled malignancy, while listening to the perfect, stubborn chug-chugging cadence of the diesel engine.

Returning to his station on the assembly line, Yuri resumed his work from where he had left off in the morning, unconcerned about hunger thanks to his lightness of heart. As the workday drew to a close, his supervisor appeared again. Startled by the unexpected visit, Yuri anticipated a word of praise or perhaps even a gesture of recognition—maybe an invitation once again to meet the photographers from the press.

The supervisor gestured for Yuri to follow without the courtesy of uttering a word. *I don't think he has said more than five words since I've begun working here.* They navigated the maze of the factory floor. When passing the quality control team, he felt their eyes boring into him. They knew the factory culture, anticipated Yuri's misfortune, and relished the spectacle of him being led away.

A bird flitted high among the iron rafters, darting aimlessly, trapped, and out of place. Yuri watched it for a moment. *It could be that it all turns out fine. Maybe not. It feels like odds are against me. . . . No photographers anywhere, I see.*

Eventually, they arrived at the office of someone important.

Without explanation, Yuri was left in the reception area while his supervisor made a hasty retreat, not speaking a word and avoiding Yuri's questioning glance.

Time dragged on. The secretary hammered away violently at her typewriter, the sound drilling into Yuri's head. Her face, with its compressed red lips and expressionless eyes, seemed chiseled from granite, betraying neither recognition nor interest in his presence. She was all business, all efficiency. No wasted motion. No squandered emotion.

Yuri slumped in his seat, feeling like a trapped animal—captured by the organs of Zetor, unable to fly, and unsure how to fight. The day began in gloom, brought a fleeting triumph, only to end in humiliation—like a soldier being drummed out of service, his brass buttons and medals stripped away.

On a bookcase, alongside a row of small Zetor tractor miniatures, hung yet another image of Gustáv Husák. The face, once regarded as avuncular, now held an unfriendly edge. Acrid cigarette smoke seeped through the cracks around the department head's office door, beneath the name "Jakub Pivnik" etched in glass.

The bird Yuri had observed earlier was now perched on a guardrail outside the office window. It cocked its head sharply, looking at him with unblinking eyes, as if to say, "You look out of place." Yuri whispered, "Go now, little bird. Fly off, before trouble comes." The typewriter paused. The secretary looked at him with an expressionless face before resuming her typing.

The secretary received a message through her intercom. Annoyed, rising stiffly, she opened the door without a ray of emotion and motioned for Yuri to enter.

"Have a seat, Mr. Dvořák," said Pivnik, his smile thin and cold. "This is Comrade Sokol—Party secretary at the Zetor plant. He's here to observe our little talk."

Yuri observed the tall man in the shadows. He had never encountered a party officer in person: stern of expression, heavyset of frame, clad in a drab uniform adorned with communist insignia. The tip of his cigarette glowed as he took a long pull, illuminating his hawk-like features. He didn't speak, didn't nod, nor did he offer any gesture of acknowledgment. Through the smoke, he peered with eyes that held an expression like one who had long ago tasted the fruit of the tree of the knowledge of good and evil.

Pivnik went on. "I'm told you got a written reprimand yesterday—something about poor workmanship. Then today during lunch, you wandered off to a station that's not yours and started working where you weren't told to. Do you care to explain that?" He spoke with clipped words, sharp consonants. He made an effort to rein in the pace of his speech.

"Yesterday they blamed me for bad work," Yuri said. "But I looked at it again. It wasn't my fault. Today, during lunch, I checked the dead tractors and saw the real trouble. Quality control made the wrong call. . . . Or maybe something worse happened."

A new thought had struck him. *What if it wasn't a mistake at all? They point the finger at me, but the real trouble came from Cab and Operator Controls. I know those guys. I worked with them. There's no way they would mess that up, not by accident.*

The expression of the man in the shadows darkened, as if he were reading Yuri's thoughts.

Pivnik paused, digesting the explanation. At first glance, Yuri's country accent and sing-song cadence might have suggested a lack of sophistication or intelligence. Perhaps it also explained why his words outran his judgment. Yet, the facts of what Yuri accomplished astonished him.

Yuri attempted to gauge Pivnik's reaction. *I said what needed saying. That should've fixed it. Why wouldn't he care? I found the problem—on the floor, where it starts. Sooner or later, it would land on his desk.*

Pivnik responded, glancing nervously at Sokol, "You didn't just find the problem, but you also took it upon yourself to correct it. I've heard your family came off a *kolkhoz* near Třeboň. That explains a few things. The standards in Brno are—how shall I say—more rigorous. Our ways are not the same as yours. Discipline here is not a suggestion. And I've found that those from the countryside often carry certain small-minded loyalties, certain petty-bourgeois habits. Old reflexes. Hard to train out."

Yuri furrowed his brow in confusion. "I don't know." *Bourgeois habits? From a collective farm worker?* His hands clenched in his lap, concealed from view.

Pivnik pressed on. "Comrade Sokol and I carry the burden of keeping party discipline at Zetor." He let a dramatic pause carry its weight. "Your actions today could be seen as a challenge to that authority. Your disregard for our party discipline establishes a dangerous precedent."

Pivnik's voice rose. "Our job is to hold the Party line—to keep unity, keep order. Yet your efforts to absolve yourself from blame on the factory floor seem to prioritize your interests and reputation over the collective good. This spirit of individualism jeopardizes the unity we work so hard to maintain. Personal ambition and self-serving actions contradict the collective ideals that should guide this factory and our work."

Yuri began feeling divided. He thought of himself as grounded in the communist faith, but he couldn't concede that what he had done was wrong. *I wasn't only thinking of myself. I wanted to help. The factory. The men who work it. People like you.*

"Yes, sir," Yuri replied, his tone flat. He felt himself becoming angry.

Pivnik continued as if the words had been memorized and rehearsed for effect. "What you did also offends the workers. You singled out the work of two teams and broke trust. That's division. Without trust, there's no equality. And without equality, we don't serve socialism—we drift toward the sickness of capitalism and the capitalist world to the west."

Yuri began to believe that communist ideals were unlikely to yield better tractors. The divide was widening, and he felt he did not want to play their game. He eventually replied, "Yes, sir."

Pivnik paused, studying Yuri with a curious expression and wondering about the long pauses between his responses. *Maybe he is a simpleton.* Then, almost reluctantly, glancing at the man in the corner, Pivnik said, "We're giving you a choice. Take a demotion. For someone like you, new here, that means off the line. You'd be cleaning floors. Toilets. That sort of thing. Or, you join the ČSM."

Yuri questioned, "The ČSM, sir?"

"It's the Czechoslovak Union of Youth," his tone implying that this was common knowledge.

In the corner, Sokol pulled again on his cigarette, the glowing ember illuminating an expression of the superiority of a master who has finally tamed his unruly dog.

47

ČSM

MIDWINTER, 1972

Petra held two wax paper sandwich bags, clinging to a little optimism as spring approached. One bag held a few tomato seeds, while the other held bush beans—gifts from her classmates. Before her lay everything she needed to start the seeds: terracotta pots, compost, topsoil, and a small watering can. She glanced at the confines of the apartment balcony, her mind wandering back to the wide-open fields of the collective farm. She looked at her hands, once calloused and strong from labor, now delicately cradling the tiny seeds. *Yuri will help me build a small garden*, thinking that the distraction of work would lift his mood.

Yuri entered the room with the day's mail, tearing open a package marked with the emblem of the ČSM and studying the contents. "It seems the local authorities have approved my application."

"Congratulations, comrade Yuri! You don't sound happy," Petra remarked. Yuri forced a smile. He had been trying to forget about it.

It was Saturday morning. Václav was away, and Zofia was immersed in a transcribed book: *The Master and Margarita*. She carefully closed the book, looked straight ahead, and her nostrils flared as she realized the implications of Yuri's decision to join the ČSM.

Her questioning gaze at Yuri was a potent rebuke. He ignored the swelling thundercloud and tried to lift the mood with mock severity. "Zofia, you'd better stay on my good side!" Then, pretending to be a secret police agent and bowing to look at her bookshelf, he said, "Ah, look at this. You have five copies of the *Selected Speeches of Klement Gottwald*. Very nice. Nothing to see here."

Zofia responded coldly, "I'm not discussing my books with anyone. If only I could hope for the same from other family members."

Yuri turned away from her reproachful glare. The memory of the smoke-filled office at Zetor resurfaced in his mind. He wondered if accepting a demotion at Zetor would have been preferable to the distrust he saw in Zofia's eyes. He hadn't foreseen these outside forces poised to tear away at family trust.

Meeting her gaze, her dark eyes fixed on him with intensity, Yuri spoke meekly. "I'll never say anything about your books."

Petra laughed, "You're not a very good communist."

Yuri's mind drifted to another time, to a cottage hidden among the trees, where someone had spoken those same words. *I'd better become a good communist if I'm to join the ČSM.*

Zofia's gaze lingered on Yuri for a moment before she returned to her book, leaving the tension between them unresolved. *And it will never happen if I let myself be held captive by her moods*, Yuri thought.

Turning his attention back to the ČSM mail package, he said, "It looks like there's a meeting tonight." He said it aloud to cement the decision for himself and to avoid appearing bested by Zofia.

The Lišeň Cultural Center was nearby, just a short walk beyond the ravine and across a bridge over the transit rail line. Yuri bundled himself against the January cold as light snow fell, blanketing the dull winter landscape in white. The snowfall softened the sounds of the city. He walked in the footprints left by others from the *byt* complex.

Upon entering the building, he followed the sound of unfamiliar voices echoing off the wooden floors. In the dimly lit halls, propaganda posters proclaiming "Youth for Peace!" and "Forward for Socialism!" failed to stir any enthusiasm within him. It rather produced an unexpected sorrow. Eventually, he found a large gathering hall with chairs and tables.

Although the package in the mail did not specify when he should start attending, Yuri decided to come anyway. No one had been informed of his arrival, and no one greeted him or introduced him to others. He acted as if he belonged, avoiding eye contact and wishing to remain invisible. He approached a table, where kettles of hot water sat simmering on electric plates, meant for tea or *Melta*, a coffee substitute. He passed over the plate of cookies; he had no appetite.

As Yuri sipped his chicory drink, he replayed the events that had led him to this moment. *A doubter can't be too careful.* Amused by the intrusion of this rebellious notion and acutely aware that skepticism would be difficult to hide, he kept a neutral expression. His strategy: linger on the fringes, bide his time, and resort to deception when necessary. Standing in the shadow of a support beam, he recalled the circumstances that had brought him to this place and the enigmatic Svoboda Sokol.

He was not as invisible. Alert and watchful, Sabrina noticed him as soon as he entered. While chatting with friends, she followed him with her eyes, noting the confidence of his movements, the strength of his broad shoulders, and the guarded expression in his eyes. Excusing herself, she crossed the room toward his table. Josef, standing nearby, observed her path.

"Hi, I remember you, I think. I'm Sabrina." The faint smell of cigarette smoke clung to her clothing.

After noticing her approach, Yuri recalled their brief encounter on his first day in Brno. He looked up at her, keeping his emotions in check. He indeed remembered. Despite his efforts, she could read what he intended to conceal.

Sabrina was captivated by the clarity in Yuri's eyes and his uncommon vigor—a striking contrast to the young men in the city. She also noticed his tension and that his well-worn, rural clothing appeared out of place.

Resigned to being discovered, Yuri stood, met her gaze, and responded, "Hi, I do remember you . . . the *fotbol* game, and you helped us move in. . . . I'm Yuri Dvořák. It's a pleasure to make your acquaintance again." He tried to recall the manners his mother had taught him. She suppressed laughter at his awkward formality.

They engaged in casual conversation, though Yuri maintained a policy of restraint, almost to the point of rudeness. To his surprise, Sabrina became less reserved as they spoke. While he offered fewer words, she became eager to engage. Through her openness, he gathered valuable information about upcoming events, activities, and campaigns, making her position of influence and leadership within the ČSM unmistakable.

Sabrina sensed the conversation had run its course. She excused herself with a friendly smile. As she walked away, she reflected on the unspoken exchange that had taken place between them. Yuri pretended not to be affected by this conversation, yet watched her depart from the corner of his eye, impressed by her tall frame. He thought of her parting words, which included an invitation to join the men's soccer team in early spring. He noticed his opinion of the ČSM beginning to improve. But he couldn't stay optimistic. The memory of Zofia's dark-eyed reproach from the previous night put him in a less favorable frame of mind.

The meeting, led by communist officials, droned on. That evening, the discussion centered on events and activities planned for the upcoming year. However, despite the free flow of conversation, everything remained within the confines of the party's priorities. Democratic decision-making was merely an illusion. Someone proposed expanding a local theater project, but the idea was quickly dismantled according to Central Committee guidelines. Another member suggested a new educational initiative, yet it was carefully worded to ensure no deviation from Marxist-Leninist principles.

As the meeting drew to a close, officials invited youth representatives to discuss the final agenda items. Sabrina stood up and introduced Yuri, along with several other new members of the ČSM. She announced that an induction ceremony was scheduled for March. *An induction ceremony?* Yuri wondered, feeling caught off guard.

Sabrina detailed the ceremony, highlighting symbolic gestures like raising a clenched fist and pinning party insignia. While she spoke, envelopes containing the loyalty oath were handed out to each new member. *Another envelope. Now I have two envelopes. I wish I had none.*

The meeting concluded, and some attendees stayed to mingle. A few individuals introduced themselves to Yuri, and for the first time, he noticed that many wore party pins.

Josef approached and straddled a seat next to Yuri, his presence causing others to drift away. He was a large young man, towering at six feet two inches, with a robust build, broad shoulders, and a strong jawline. His neatly combed hair swept straight back, and his party pin shone with an almost tangible intensity. Smiling, he introduced himself.

Josef spoke glibly about numerous topics, most of which Yuri either didn't understand or soon forgot. His demeanor was friendly—perhaps too friendly—and his eyes sparkled with a hint of madness. Yuri felt he could never measure up to the high standards of the New Faith. He had never encountered anyone like Josef on the collective farm and struggled to find words to respond, lacking the vocabulary to keep up.

Exhausted by his expenditure of words, Josef suddenly shifted gears, pressing Yuri about his job. The abrupt change caught Yuri off guard, prompting him to offer a vague, terse response.

Unable to contain himself at this trivial affront, Josef blurted out, "I heard a rumor that you were reprimanded at Zetor." The conversation lapsed into an awkward silence. Yuri had never experienced such a change from friendliness to hostility.

Yuri felt his passion rise. For an instant, his composure faltered. *How does he know? Who told him?* Yuri began to realize that privacy in the city was a fragile illusion. He noticed Sabrina chatting with a friend, but her occasional glances toward the unfolding spectacle suggested she was acutely aware of the tension between them.

Josef stayed unnervingly composed. "Loyalty means everything to us, Yuri. But I wonder—are you here tonight out of conviction or necessity?" Then, with a menacing smile, Josef added, "You even look like a Christian. I hear collective farms are breeding grounds for religious fervor."

The remark carried a hint of menace, but though Yuri felt the sting, he kept a cool head. A memory flashed through his mind—images from a magazine article featuring photographs of Nazi leaders. Without hesitation, Yuri responded, "Pardon my bluntness, but you look an awful lot like Hermann Göring. You must be related, no?"

Yuri's quick response caught Josef off guard, cutting like a sword. Blood rushed to Josef's face, his jaw tightening as he abruptly stood, sending his chair crashing backward. He faced Yuri, his fingers curling into fists. Conversations in the hall fell silent, and all eyes turned to them.

Yuri controlled his breathing as he slowly rose from his seat and took his stand. He fixed his gaze on Josef, a cautious smile spreading across his face. *His madness is confirmed. Well then, let the excitement begin.*

The tension hung in the air, but Josef backed down and left the scene.

Yuri thought, *So much for keeping a low profile tonight. There's no fringe left for me to linger in,* as he noticed the remaining attendees still staring at him. He decided it was time to leave. With a heavy heart, he put on his coat, discarded his cup, strode past the propaganda posters without a second thought, and stepped outside, taking a deep breath of the cool air. He checked to make sure he hadn't forgotten his envelope.

RETROSPECTIVE

MIDWINTER, 1972

Yuri found his coat and slipped out of the Lisen Cultural Center. It was 9:30 P.M., and the snowfall had stopped. A pale, orange moon rose, occasionally breaking through fragments of cloud as the temperature dropped. After crossing back over the transit line rails, Yuri entered the park-like ravine. In solitude, he wandered, reflecting on all that had transpired.

Before long, his gaze fell upon a man tenderly guiding his mentally disabled son. It was difficult to determine the boy's age; he might have been in his teens. They were engaged in a playful, late-evening snowball fight in the thin layer of snow. The boy's peculiar laughter rang out merrily as he tried to make a snowball, only to crumble in his hands before he could launch it. Then, his father would run up behind him, popping him in the back with a soft snowball, causing the boy to collapse onto the snow in a fit of laughter.

The father approached again, holding another snowball. The boy, now covered in snow, got up to grasp and hug him, a gesture of surrender. His father dropped the snowball, brushed the snow off his gloves, and gently stroked his son's head. After a moment, they departed together, glove in glove.

Yuri continued to wander, his mind still troubled by the events at the ČSM, made still more so by the scene he had just now witnessed. Brushing the snow off a park bench, he sat down, resting his head in his hands. The envelope containing the loyalty oath was pressed against his chest inside his coat. His thoughts turned to Father Kaleda and his mysterious envelope. *Now I have two envelopes. What would Kaleda think of my loyalty oath?*

He imagined the blind priest sitting beside him, his calm voice pressing gently: *"Did you see the love of that father for his handicapped son? Tell me, Yuri, what do you think? Was it not a beautiful thing to behold? And where would this poor boy be if his father had been loyal to communism? That's right. The son would be deemed useless to the glorious socialist state, and they would place him in an institution to rot. Who loves you, Yuri? Karl Marx? Klement Gottwald, Svoboda Sokol? Do they love you more than your father, more than your sisters, or even more than I do? Tell me, does love break into your family affairs to frighten you? To make you hide a book? To cause you to distrust friends and even family? To spy on you? To punish you for doing your work too well?*

"And your new acquaintance, Josef—is he what you wish to become? He mocks you, questions your loyalty. Maybe he's right. Perhaps your loyalty is starting to waver. I hope it is.

"By the way, you now have another envelope. What will you do?"

Yuri recalled Father Kaleda's words from his youth as he warned his congregation against atheistic indoctrination, quoting Jesus: "'Whoever is not with me is against me. And whoever does not gather with me scatters.'"

His mind drifted to the provocation that had nearly erupted into a brawl. *He's a madman. I almost wish he'd thrown the first punch.* His adrenaline subsided as he thought of his mother.

Yuri returned to the apartment, closing the door softly behind him. In an attempt to appear relaxed, he picked up a random magazine, took a seat across from Zofia, and pretended to read it. Her eyes drifted between the pages of her "propaganda" book and the figure seated across from her. After a moment, she closed her book and broke the silence.

"Okay, what's the matter?"

Yuri glanced up briefly. "What? How do you know something's the matter?"

She replied with a bland expression, "Do you need to ask?"

Ignoring the comment, Yuri flipped a page, feigning interest in the magazine. She held him with her eyes. *Why can't I come home and sit in peace without those eyes on me?*

Attempting to change the subject, he asked, "What are you reading tonight?"

Zofia set her book down with deliberation but said nothing. Yuri raised his hands in a gesture of surrender. Finally, he began to talk about the evening and Josef.

"I don't understand why he singled me out. . . ."

"Yuri," she began, "he somehow knew about your reprimand at Zetor. But why would he care?"

"Yeah, he's questioning my loyalty to communism," Yuri replied.

Zofia's dark hair fell across her face as she lowered her head, looked askance at him, and asked, "Well, are you? . . . Loyal, that is?"

Feeling cornered, Yuri recognized her deft maneuver and replied in an annoyed tone, "Loyalty? I don't know. I go to the meetings so I can keep my job. That's all." He did not want to admit his growing doubts, especially to her. He was ready for the conversation to end.

Unimpressed by his weak response, she declared, "Well, what are you? You can't sit on two chairs."

Deflecting the question, Yuri said, "I don't know why Josef would care. Honestly, I don't know why anyone cares."

Zofia responded with some intensity, her annoyance returning, "I care. It matters to me whether I can trust you."

Eager to intervene and ward off another confrontation, Petra cut in bluntly, "One thing's for sure—he wants you gone. It's probably because of a girl."

All three paused, trying to make sense of this new possibility.

Zofia broke the silence, "I remember our first day in Brno when that group of *fotbal* players met us at the train stop. I couldn't help but notice Sabrina's interest in you . . . Josef didn't miss that either. Did you speak to her tonight?"

Yuri nodded, "Yes, I spoke to her. . . . It's a possibility anyway." He hesitated and added thoughtfully, "Maybe. But I think there's more to it. He seemed so . . . zealous and angry." Petra cast a glance at Yuri, gauging his reaction to the mention of her name.

Zofia stood up abruptly. "Well, I hope Josef continues to plague you if it keeps you away from that girl. She's trouble." Without waiting for a reply, she marched off to her bedroom, hugging her book to her chest. Yuri considered her words. It hadn't occurred to him to distrust Sabrina. *"She's trouble." Hadn't I once thought that about Sabrina?*

Petra bid goodnight to Yuri and their father before following Zofia. Despite their efforts to be discreet, Yuri could hear the faint sound of their whispered, agitated conversation behind the closed door.

Václav invited Yuri to stay and talk. After a few moments of silence, he spoke softly, "I need to tell you something, but you must promise not to tell the girls."

"I promise," Yuri replied.

"I'm planning something I can't tell you," Václav continued. "That's why I've been away so much in the evenings. For your safety, you shouldn't know the details. Trust me. If something goes wrong when these plans are executed, I've arranged for Jaroslav Krčméry in Třeboň to take in Zofia and Petra. I'm also working to get them travel permits, but it's proving difficult."

"You're doing what?" Yuri asked.

"I'm planning something. It must be kept secret. You'll know when the time is right."

"You made plans for the girls, but what about me?" Yuri asked.

"I can't include you. Krčméry doesn't have the space, and adding you to the permit would attract too much attention from the authorities. You have your job, and your lack of knowledge about my plans should be enough to keep you out of trouble. But this won't be a walk in a rose garden."

Yuri sighed, his frustration barely contained. "Is this why we left Třeboň?" he asked, irritation rising in his voice.

"I'm sorry, son. I wish I could tell you more. I hope it will all make sense one day, and you'll be proud of me. Good night," Václav said as he prepared to retire.

"Wait, *Táta*," Yuri said, rising from his seat. Remembering what he had witnessed in the ravine, he embraced his father. It had been a long time.

Yuri sat alone. His father's words filled him with melancholy. Resentment toward the New Faith settled over him. Zofia's disapproval weighed on him. He fumbled with the envelope in his pocket, hesitant to open it. On the table before him lay a trade magazine, *Práce*, that only his father would read. We would have normally ignored it. Now he especially viewed it with an utter lack of interest. It was a magazine aligned with the Communist Party, not representing workers to management, but rather the Party's concerns to the workers. Nevertheless, he picked it up and flipped through it, agitated— delaying the moment he would read the envelope, and the sleeplessness and aching conscience that would follow. He found a dog-eared page of stories that were subtle warnings. Workers at Škoda Works who attempted to "disrupt production" were accused of having "failed in their socialist duty." *Why did he dog-ear this page?*

The idea of withdrawing from the ČSM crossed his mind, along with its potential consequences—the most serious being increased surveillance of their family. Yet, considering his father's plans, whatever they were, leaving was no longer an option.

Yuri felt drawn toward a compromise: outwardly conforming to communist ideology while inwardly distancing himself from its principles. For the sake of his family, he began to resolve that he would play the role expected of him. *I'll take the loyalty oath. I'll wear the pin. I'll look loyal. I'll do what they expect.*

He opened the envelope given to him at the meeting and found the loyalty oath. It read:

```
     "I, Yuri Dvořák, solemnly pledge
my loyalty and allegiance to the
Communist Party of Czechoslovakia and
to the socialist state. As a member of
the Československý svaz mládeže, I vow
to uphold the principles of Marxism-
Leninism and to work tirelessly for the
advancement of communism. I will strive
to promote social justice, equality, and
solidarity among all people. I pledge to
actively participate in the activities
```

```
of the ČSM, to support its goals, and to
contribute to the building of a socialist
society based on the ideals of collective
effort and cooperation. I understand that
by taking this oath, I become a part
of a unified community of young adults
dedicated to the cause of communism and
the betterment of our nation. So help me,
comrades."
```

He replaced the contents of the envelope. Father Kaleda spoke through his conscience: "Let your 'yes' be yes, and your 'no' be no." He felt the tension between the loyalty oath's demands and the mystery of Father Kaleda's envelope. *I may be holding the family together, but I feel like I'm breaking apart.*

SERGEI

MIDWINTER, 1972

"Turn up the volume; I like the Beatles," Petra said to Zofia, who was holding a small, boxy transistor radio to her ear.

"It will be a bother. Sit closer if you want to hear—I don't mind."

The tram slowed to a stop. Passengers from the Krásného tram stop boarded, including Sergei. Petra stole a glance at Zofia, noting her forced composure and the quiet click of the radio being switched off.

Petra leaned in and whispered as if she were ignorant, "I like that Beatles song. Do you think the radio will bother people? . . . Or just a certain person, mmm?" Petra received an elbow in her side.

"*Dobré ráno*," Sergei greeted Zofia and Petra as he stood near them. The tram was too crowded for a seat. Both noticed his fine clothes and kind smile.

"*Dobré ráno*," they replied—Petra with cheerful openness, Zofia a bit too politely.

"*As-tu fini tes devoirs?*" Sergei asked Zofia.

"Uhhh, *Oui, je l'ai fini*," she replied clumsily, after some thought.

Petra protested, "Clever. You both have your little private language." Another elbow jabbed her side; this time, less subtle, less gentle.

Unable to leave her sister in suspense, Zofia said, "He just asked me if I finished my homework. I said that I had." Sergei smiled at the drama.

Petra whispered in reply, "Oh, thanks—perfectly explains my bruised ribs."

As Zofia and Sergei chatted casually, Petra noticed the older people seated nearby stiffen at the sound of Sergei's German accent and steal disapproving glances. The memory of the German occupation still lingered.

After the tram veered northwest and turned south, they all disembarked at the Lesnická tram stop. Petra left the other two waiting for a trolley bus while she hurried off to Mendel University of Agriculture and Forestry. Glancing over her shoulder, she called out, "Sorry, I'm late. *Na shledanou.*"

"*Na shledanou*," Zofia and Sergei replied.

Zofia and Sergei boarded the trolley bus for a short ride to the Brno State Language School. Before heading to their classrooms, Sergei said, "The weather is perfect for enjoying the outdoors. Would you like to meet me at lunch for a walk to Špilberk Castle?"

With graceful reserve, she replied, "Yes."

How can he say the weather is perfect? It's terrible, she thought.

With the temperature warming to 6°C and recent rains, a dense fog enveloped the city. Zigzagging their way south past terraced buildings, Zofia lost her sense of direction and became uncomfortably reliant on Sergei. Sycamore trees lined the streets, their bare branches towering above and partially obscured by the mist. They walked across centuries-old cobblestones arranged in a herringbone pattern. She gazed at other couples holding hands. Coming from the farm, where everyone knew everything about her, she experienced the peculiar delight of being unknown and unnoticed.

They arrived at Café Podnebí, near the entrance to the castle grounds. Inside, they chose a table by a tall window overlooking the gently sloping paths ascending toward Špilberk Castle. A radiator beside them emitted warmth, its metal ticking and popping softly. After placing their orders, they were served steaming bowls of potato soup and cups of coffee.

Sergei was respectful and attentive to Zofia. She remained composed and polite, governing her emotions. However, she felt self-conscious and off balance. Coming from the countryside, she was unfamiliar with how to "read" young men in the city. At home, the boys were predictable and clumsy in her presence. Sergei, however, was not clumsy and unafraid to speak to her, which made her both wary and intrigued.

"How are you managing your verb conjugations?" Sergei asked, with deliberate clumsiness to set her at ease.

"It's maddening trying to learn the irregular verbs. Does it ever get easier?" she replied.

"I think you're doing very well. You have a gift, judging by how quickly you've picked up the pronunciation. I'd be happy to practice with you . . . anytime," he answered casually, looking away.

Zofia stared into her soup, weighing his words. After a moment, she asked, "You speak Czech fluently. Where did you learn the language so well?"

"I grew up in Vienna, Austria. My *Táta* was a business executive at the Grand Hotel Wien, and my *Maminka* was a doctor. Her family came from Czechoslovakia, from a small town called Dolní Věstonice, just north of Vienna. I was an only child and was often left alone after school. Every summer, they sent me north from the city—and from their lives—to stay with her brother, who owned a vineyard. So I grew up speaking both languages."

Zofia struggled to suppress her feelings for him. He spoke plainly, not seeking pity. She felt it nonetheless. Her father's warnings echoed in her mind as she attempted to look past Sergei's charm. Yet her conscience faltered, and his wealth and striking appearance did little to steady her reserve.

"So you live alone in Brno?" she asked.

"Yes."

Her breath caught. What had she just said? She looked down and stirred her soup, which was growing cold.

Sergei, confused by her reaction, broke the silence. "Tell me about your family, Zofia."

Zofia gave a brief history of their childhood home in Kolence, the forced sale of their family farm to the State, and the move to the collective farm in Třeboň. She told of her *Maminka*'s death, the pain of her loss, and the recent, abrupt decision for their whole family to move to Brno. Sergei already knew Petra, but he was surprised to learn she had a brother.

"And tell me about Yuri."

Zofia finished her description of Yuri by adding, "He can be a devil if he's provoked. Here's just one example. . . ." She told Sergei about the incident in the cafeteria, of the uncouth boy who mouthed off, embarrassing her, and how he met with the full wrath of her brother.

Wanting to express her admiration for what Yuri had done, she shifted back in time and continued describing the aftermath of the incident. . . .

Zofia skipped the extracurricular activities and went straight home after school. Tearfully, she removed her homemade dress, vowing never to wear it again, and put on the approved costume. The dress lay crumpled on the floor, and in her anger, she kicked it. Standing in front of the mirror, she wiped away her tears. Vojta's words stung with a hint of truth. She also realized she belonged to the world "out there," beyond the farm, where a girl could wear stylish clothes without facing provocative comments from stupid farm boys.

She called for Yuri, but when he didn't answer, she ran to the mechanic's shop and stood in the doorway, quietly watching him work.

A disemboweled Zetor tractor was parked at one end of the shop. Wrenches of various sizes were scattered across the floor or hanging from the walls. Benches were cluttered with belts, cans of fluid, and boxes of tools. Oil mixed with rainwater collected in one corner of the shop. The strong smell of oil and diesel fuel lingered in the air. Light from the afternoon sun streamed in through the western windows. Her father and brother worked together to reconnect the drive shaft to the transmission of a tractor.

This world felt foreign and mysterious to Zofia as she watched and leaned against the doorpost as if to hide. Her countenance toward him had improved since the morning. She also understood that harsh consequences loomed for Yuri on her account.

Yuri looked up at the silhouette in the doorway. Once his eyes adjusted to the light, they met hers. The wind blew steadily, sweeping her dark hair across her face. She swiftly turned and walked away.

. . . Sergei considered for a little time what kind of relationship she had with her brother. *He is a protector, a fighter, and only a* mechanic. Returning to the present, he said, "And why are you studying French?"

After some reflection, she said, "I love reading. I hope to enjoy French literature someday, and I'm charmed by the elegance and beauty of the language."

"What books do you like to read?"

Zofia's words trotted out, "I don't have many books—*The Master and Margarita, Animal Farm, 1984,* to name a few."

"Do you *own* these books?" he asked, mildly surprised.

With a hint of pride, she replied, "Sort of. I transcribed them from the books that friends owned when we lived in Třeboň."

She fell silent as blood rushed to her face. The weight of her admission hit her, revealing something she had sworn to keep secret. Tears began to rise, and she fought to command them back to their source.

Sergei held her gaze for a fraction of a second too long, his expression unreadable. He took a slow sip of coffee before finally saying, "Are you okay? You're taking a risk by owning these books, you know. I'll keep this secret if that's your concern. . . . I can't believe you transcribed so many books."

Zofia grew quiet, her mind disturbed. She offered terse responses to Sergei's patient questions, giving answers calculated to check rather than encourage inquiry. She wished she could be back in Třeboň. She wished she could disappear into a hole. And yet, she thought, with both vexation and reluctant admiration, that he read her mood perfectly.

Their plans to walk the castle grounds were cut short. She left her soup untouched, and they returned to the language school. As she neared the college, Zofia's embarrassment melted away, though she felt annoyed at having to rely on Sergei to lead the way back. Sergei chatted casually beside her as if nothing had happened. She stole occasional glances at him but avoided meeting his eye.

When they parted, Zofia straightened her back and calmly bid him farewell. As she walked away, her expression fell just short of a smile, but inside, an unfamiliar, dangerous pride remained unchecked.

The fog blurred the outlines of campus buildings as she ran up the stairs.

GAME DAY

EARLY SPRING, 1972

Winter gave way to spring in Brno, Czechoslovakia. The icy fingers of the season loosened their grip on the city, and the grass of the Líšeň ravine turned vibrant green under the growing warmth of the sun. The earth was glad, and the trees rejoiced. The sweet fragrance of lilacs drifted through open windows, beckoning winter-weary inhabitants to step outside.

Youth from the ČSM—young men and women alike—poured onto the field. Some emerged from nearby apartments, while others arrived by tram. A few carried thermoses and poured their contents into small cups, warming their hands. Some came reluctantly; after all, it was a Party-organized event. Dressed for *fotbal*, they ignored the sting of cold on their exposed arms and legs. Soccer balls appeared—one, then two, then three—arcing between players, occasionally running under close control, as their owners maneuvered past imaginary opponents.

Yuri stepped onto the ravine, his breath visible in the chilly air. He was eager for competition, but he measured the skill of the other athletes and was not encouraged. Farm life had allowed little time for recreation.

Zofia arrived later, wrapped in warmer clothes, to watch the game.

A red Škoda 1000 MB pulled up next to the field, attracting the athletes' attention. Automobiles were a rare sight, reserved for the privileged. Sabrina stepped out, clearly embarrassed. A couple of friends ran to greet her. Yuri tried to peer at the driver through the car's window, but the face remained obscured. He remembered that this car model was favored among government officials. Sabrina scanned the field, noting who had arrived, while Yuri casually turned away in a game of concealment, not wanting to look too interested.

After considerable debate, the thirteen young men were divided into two teams based on their perceived strengths. The new ČSM inductees, including Yuri, were chosen last. Meanwhile, the girls, forming their teams, were more verbal and careful not to offend. After forming their teams, the young men walked past the huddled girls, still immersed in conversation, and took to the field.

"Don't let the sun go down before you play," one of the guys said as he passed. The girls fell silent with annoyed expressions, glancing over their shoulders as the boys passed. Yuri walked by Sabrina and shrugged as though ignorant of what was meant.

Josef arrived late on his motor scooter. The huddled girls stifled their laughter as the large youth puttered slowly onto the field on the diminutive, almost feminine vehicle. Thinking like a mechanic, Yuri wondered how such a small engine could carry such a massive bulk. *Something sounds wrong with that scooter.*

After reluctantly shedding layers, the games began. The players fought through stiff limbs and clumsy movements—passes went astray, shots lacked power, bodies collided, and lungs burned. But as the games wore on, the cold no longer mattered.

A young girl gravitated toward Zofia, who followed after Yuri. Sitting beside her and looking up with searching eyes, the girl decided she wanted to be her friend. She had wafer cookies in her pocket, bound together with a rubber band. Zofia, intently watching the games, didn't notice her new companion. The little girl put her hand on Zofia's arm and introduced herself, offering a wafer cookie to win her friendship. Charmed by the bribe, Zofia forgot about the game and turned her attention to this new friend. As the girl shared the details of her lonely life, Zofia listened with sympathetic eyes, absorbed in her story. Unaccustomed to a listening ear and mesmerized by Zofia's beauty, the girl overwhelmed her with a torrent of words.

Petra arrived and sat beside Zofia, opposite the little girl, ignoring the game. She remarked, "What a beautiful day! How I wish I were back in Třeboň now, getting the fields ready instead of just sitting around. How is Yuri doing?"

Zofia pointed toward the field, pretending to have followed the game. "See him there? Playing defense? That big guy is Josef. Remember him from our first day? He keeps charging through the defense like an ox, right past Yuri. At one point, Yuri grabbed his jersey and pulled him to the ground. Not the best way to improve their relationship—it almost started a brawl between the two teams. Oh, meet my little friend, Ivana. She claims she likes books. We're having a parley."

Petra brightened and introduced herself to Ivana, "Ooo, a parley! What's this parley about? Are you certain Zofia isn't planning a 'party' instead?"

With cookie crumbs encrusted around her mouth, Ivana spoke innocently with a gentle, sweet lilt, "I have the book *The Lord of the Rings*, but no one will read it to me. My parents are too busy. Zofia said that it's probably a book I shouldn't have, but she also said she would read it to me." Ivana smiled, deciding that she liked Petra, too. Zofia tensed, suddenly rethinking what she had promised, both for its risk and Petra's inevitable reaction.

Petra's eyes widened as she turned to Zofia, her expression conveying, *Are you sure you know what you're doing?* Then, turning playfully to Ivana, she said, "You need to be careful about whom you choose as friends. Zofia sometimes breaks the rules. . . .”

Ivana giggled. This transgressive secret with the "big girls" held a special charm for her.

Zofia said, "She's so sweet—and so lonely. I could eat her up. Her parents are often away. She mentioned that the book was a gift from them, and she keeps it well hidden.”

Ivana scrunched her nose. "Are you going to eat me up?”

Petra added, "I'm concerned about you two reading it together. Why invite trouble?”

Their conversation was interrupted as their attention shifted to the game. Yuri chased a ball that had rolled out of bounds into the girls' field. They watched him exchange a few words with Sabrina, followed by a shared laugh, before they went their separate ways.

Zofia and Petra exchanged raised eyebrows and knowing smiles. Zofia asked, "Is Yuri aware that he might be getting himself into trouble?”

"No more trouble than you might be walking into with Sergei,” Petra replied bluntly. Zofia's face darkened.

The games ended around the same time, and the players started to disperse. Yuri walked off the field, hanging his head because of his performance. As he reached the sidelines, Sabrina approached him.

"My father wishes to speak with you privately,” she said.

Yuri stopped and stood staring at Sabrina.

"Well, c'mon,” she coaxed.

"Okay,” he replied plainly, then followed her like a lamb to the spot where a man stood alone beside the field, smoking a cigarette. As they drew closer, Yuri's steps faltered. Recognition dawned on him, and he slowed, slightly stunned; he struggled to believe what he saw. Svoboda Sokol.

Yuri whispered to Sabrina, "He's your father?”

Puzzled by the emotion in his voice, she replied, "Of course. . . . Are you afraid?” It was too late for Yuri to change his mind about this interview. She introduced him to her father, then stepped aside, leaving them alone.

Sokol dropped his cigarette, grinding it into the grass, and the two exchanged casual greetings. For the first time, Yuri heard him speak—a low-pitched, smoky voice honed for command. Sokol's face bore scars that could frighten a child. Though months had passed since Yuri had last seen him, he found himself unexpectedly raw with emotion.

"Yuri, you received a reprimand at Zetor a few months ago for your independent spirit. You were divisive and challenged authority,”

Sokol rasped.

Yuri's attention drifted momentarily in a subconscious effort to retreat mentally. In the distance, he noticed Zofia and Petra with a little girl he didn't recognize, their gazes fixed on him. Sabrina joined them. Across the ravine, Josef struggled futilely to start his motor scooter. Nearby, red squirrels scurried about, foraging for rediscovered nuts, chattering with one another, and shaking off the stupor of their winter confinement. He took this all in quickly.

"Since you came to our attention, we have been keeping a close eye on you. We expected more trouble," Sokol continued.

"Yes, sir," Yuri replied awkwardly. Sokol stopped and fixed him with a steady wolf-like gaze, puzzled by the ambiguity of his response, unsure how to interpret it. *Two words, so many meanings.*

"We expected more trouble from you, but you've given us none. We talked about how you quickly resolved that issue with the tractor on the line. Quick thinking. Impressive. Sabrina has also told me about your studies. Your debates with the ČSM. Said you're sharp—can argue both sides, think on your feet. That's not something we often see in a factory worker."

Sokol paused, gazing into the distance with a casual expression, trying to catch Yuri off guard. "She mentioned you made a strong argument for the capitalist point of view. How did you conduct your research?"

Yuri selected his words with care. "I received help in locating resources."

Sokol stiffened slightly, his expression revealing dissatisfaction with the evasive answer, but he chose to let it go for now. "I understand your father was a major at the Battle of Sokolovo. Fought with distinction, from what I've heard. A man in that position would've commanded many. Carried weight. Does he stay in touch with any of his old comrades?"

"None that I know of, sir," Yuri replied, though his thoughts drifted to the many evenings his father was away and to the brief meeting with Miloslav. *What other details might he know about our family? Why is he asking these questions?*

Nearby, Josef had given up on trying to kick-start his motor scooter and now stood beside Sabrina, watching. Sokol paced the conversation to ensure maximum intimidation.

"Do you enjoy your work at Zetor?" Sokol rasped. "I mean, working with your hands on the assembly line."

"Yes, sir," Yuri replied, his unease deepening. He wished he could fly away.

▽

"You understand, of course, that your income will stay limited as long as you remain on the factory floor. But if you were to assume a party leadership role, your wages and privileges would increase significantly. I'm prepared to offer you my patronage, if you're willing."

Yuri remained silent, caught off guard by the unexpected shift in the conversation. The red squirrels that had been darting about earlier were nowhere in sight. Curious, he looked around and then upward. A buzzard perched in a nearby tree.

Sokol pressed on. "Before I make a formal offer, I need to address a concern from your past. You attended church with your *Maminka* and sisters about 10 years ago. Are you a Christian?"

"No, sir," Yuri replied, attempting to sound convincing.

"And one more question: you once attended a church in Kolence led by a Hussite priest named Father Kaleda. Have you had any contact with him in the years since?"

Yuri's attention shifted to a red squirrel, impatient with the imposition of confinement. It coveted a nut from the previous year's harvest, partially visible. Risking full exposure, it dashed into the open. The buzzard perched nearby dropped silently from its branch, its talons extended like sharpened arrows. The squirrel squeaked frantically as the buzzard flew off with its prey, its talons sunk deep into the creature's fur.

Yuri shuddered as the image seared into his mind—unexpected, violent, final. Controlling his fear, he lied with feigned boldness, a little too loud, "No, sir."

Sokol disregarded the spectacle unfolding nearby. Instead, he fixed his cold, penetrating gaze on Yuri, as if the incident had been conjured and orchestrated solely to test him. Yuri counted twelve heartbeats. Then Sokol spoke again, his voice resonating with authority.

"Are you willing to accept my patronage and be admitted into party leadership?"

Yuri drew a deep breath, then exhaled before replying, "Wouldn't you rather have someone who's been to college? Someone from the city, someone who knows how things work here?"

Sokol glanced at Yuri, puzzled. "Some might prefer that. I don't. City garbage. They're worse than senseless things—too obsessed with cinema. Soft. I want working-class youth, young people not yet corrupted by the city. People who know what it means to sweat. Industrious boys." Sokol paused, casting a stern glance at Yuri. "You don't need to concern yourself with my choice. I know exactly what I'm looking for."

Yuri recalled the stinging words from weeks ago, how being from the farm was seen as a liability. Whom should he now believe?

He looked at tall Sabrina from afar. The wind had picked up, sending her hair streaming behind her like a banner momentarily. His thoughts turned to the work he loved, and then to Sokol's offer—the sacrifices he might have to make, and the compromises he would need to accept. He felt a momentary warmth from the compliments given to him and his family, along with the promise of better income. Yet, Father Kaleda's warnings and rejection of communist ideology lingered in Yuri's mind. He also thought of Zofia.

Summoning his courage, he said, "If I were truly a committed communist, why offer me money to prove it? Wouldn't the reward of serving the cause be enough?"

Sokol was caught off guard by the reply, unaccustomed to hearing anything from young people that wasn't obsequious. He replied with a sharp edge of sarcasm, "Well, if you'd like, we can give you all the responsibility without the rewards."

Yuri held his ground. "You've said many kind things, and your offer's generous. I'm grateful. But I'm not sure if I should accept it. I need some time to think."

Sokol nodded, struck a match to light another cigarette, and then tossed it away with more force than necessary. "Of course," he grumbled. They exchanged parting words before Sokol walked to his red Škoda. Sabrina joined her father, smiling at Yuri as she passed, yet with questioning eyes. Moments later, the car disappeared down the road. Josef walked back to his motor scooter.

Zofia, Petra, and Ivana approached Yuri, commenting on the spectacle of the squirrel and the meeting with Sokol. What Zofia learned displeased her. She wished he had outright rejected Sokol's offer. Sensing the tension, Ivana trotted over and offered him her last wafer cookie as a gesture of comfort.

Eventually, Zofia and Petra left for their apartment, with Zofia marching ahead of her sister. Ivana scrambled to keep up with Zofia's brisk pace. Yuri stayed in the ravine, reluctant to follow. He had no desire to face Zofia when she was in such a mood.

73

JOSEF

EARLY SPRING, 1972

The wind gusted, muffling the city's clamor and giving Yuri a rare moment to listen to his soul. As he walked along the edge of the ravine, his thoughts churned. *What comes with this offer? Trouble or fortune? Should loyalty to the state outweigh my loyalty to family? Maybe I can have both. Zofia will understand if I explain it to her carefully.*

In the distance, he saw a police car with blue beacon lights pulsing. He veered onto a narrow path that climbed a low ridge. A tram rumbled by, its throaty electric buzz blending with the rolling hum of metal wheels on tracks, intruding on the quiet. Yuri continued southwest along the trail, his hands clasped behind his back, enjoying the cover of trees and the elevated view of the city below.

What does it mean that Sabrina is the daughter of a party official? The thought perplexed him. He thought favorably of her and, well, possibly wanted to know her better. *What could go wrong?* Somewhere to the north, the screech of wheels echoed as a tram navigated a curve.

Returning to the southern end of the ravine, Yuri thought he was alone until he noticed Josef slumped beside his motor scooter on the far side, his head buried in his hands. Pretending not to see him, Yuri turned and started walking toward home.

His mind wandered to Franz Kafka's *The Metamorphosis.* He thought of the story's theme, of Greta's care for her brother Gregor after his grotesque transformation into a giant insect. The moral force of the story appealed to him in vain. He pressed on, determined not to think. Father Kaleda's words came to him: "Love your enemies and pray for those who persecute you." The teaching gnawed at him. *Why do people think I'm a Christian? I'm not a Christian. Love my enemy? I hate my enemy.*

He forged ahead, determined to outpace his thoughts and to put as much distance as possible between himself and Josef, hoping distance would quiet his accusing conscience. Memories of his deepest regret invaded his thoughts—never having apologized to his mother before her death, the one person who had never harbored resentment toward anyone.

Defeated, Yuri halted. He turned and walked back toward Josef. *I'll do it for her.*

Yuri spoke in a flat, monotone voice, alarming Josef, who didn't realize he had approached. "I can try to help you fix your motor scooter."

Josef looked up, his gaze puzzled, measuring. "I don't need *your* help."

Yuri thought of the image of the giant insect. "Hate me or distrust me if you want. I might be able to help you. You have my permission to hate me still. Wait here while I grab my toolbox."

"Where else can I go? I'd carry the scooter home on my back if I could avoid seeing you again." Josef responded.

Yuri returned with two toolboxes and a cardboard box. "May I assume you're permitting me to work on your scooter?"

Josef nodded, looking away. Yuri knelt beside the scooter, methodically shutting off the fuel line and detaching the carburetor. He disassembled it and carefully placed the parts into the cardboard box. Josef, who had initially seemed indifferent, began to watch the process with growing interest.

After cleaning the components with carburetor cleaner, Yuri reassembled and reinstalled the carburetor. He turned the fuel back on and kick-started the scooter. It sputtered and ran unevenly but showed signs of life. Picking up a small screwdriver, Yuri adjusted the idle screw, throttle stop screw, and fuel mixture screw, fine-tuning the balance of air and fuel. The motor scooter sounded brand new.

Yuri stood up, wiped his hands on the grass, and, cautiously, permitted himself a moment of triumph, recalling his misfortune the last time he felt this way.

He packed his tools and prepared to leave without saying a word. Josef, now standing and listening to the steady hum of the engine, confessed, "This is my father's motor scooter. I was late for the game and took it without asking. He would have noticed by this afternoon when he woke up. It wouldn't have gone well for me, even though I saved him from breaking down at work. It doesn't matter. One way or another, I'd have been blamed. Anyway, now that the scooter is running well, better than before, he'll be left wondering what happened. He notices things; that's his job. I'll have to tell him, and he'll want to meet you. I'll be a little more direct: you must come home with me."

Yuri nodded. "I'll return my tools and meet you here. Don't go anywhere." Josef laughed at Yuri's reply, sensing that Yuri likely wished for anything but to return to this place.

When Yuri returned his tools, Zofia looked at his soiled hands and turned away without a word. He said nothing about where he was going and departed. As he walked back, it struck him that Josef had been abandoned in the ravine, with no one to help him. *Surely, among all the ČSM guys, one could have stepped up to help.*

Warning Josef to take it slow, Yuri clung to the scooter as it lugged them slowly east on Mifkova Street. They turned left onto Šimáčkova Street, then veered to the northeast. People walking the streets turned their heads to watch. Yuri gradually adjusted to the intimate seating arrangement with someone who had recently been an adversary. He forgot about it as he studied the rows of plain, two-story apartment buildings with no gaps between them, their red-tiled roofs and brick-and-stucco exteriors blending into a uniform streetscape.

As they traveled further north, the landscape began to change. Single-family homes appeared, some adorned with flower boxes. Automobiles and other motor scooters sped past them dangerously close, while a stray dog lazily snapped at their slow-moving heels. Yuri hoped for the journey to end.

He reflected on the irony of the party's rhetoric about classlessness. As they approached the city's outskirts, the disparities in housing grew more apparent. For a moment, he suspected Josef's family might belong to a higher social class—until they arrived at an aging apartment building that appeared out of place, tucked among the nicer homes.

As they parked the scooter, Yuri noticed a neighbor watching them, her narrowed eyes filled with silent reproach. In a neighborhood where car ownership was the norm, Josef's family owned only a single motor scooter. *Why did she look at us that way?*

Peering down the street, Yuri asked, "That looks like the same Škoda driven by Sabrina's father?"

"Yes," Josef replied curtly.

When they entered the lower-level apartment, Yuri immediately noticed the artifacts of lives untouched by a woman's gentle hand. His eyes adjusted to the light filtering through crooked window shutters. Dust blanketed surfaces undisturbed by daily use, worn furniture sagged, and unwashed dishes were piled in the sink. At the table, a young man—evidently Josef's brother—sat staring coldly at Yuri.

"Why did you bring *him* here?" he growled, rising abruptly and exiting the room without waiting for a response.

Yuri, unsettled by the man's malicious eyes, turned to Josef. "I think I know him."

"You do, and he knows you," Josef replied with a grim smile. "He works in quality control at Zetor."

Josef couldn't ignore the irony—the skill that had repaired his motor scooter and saved him from trouble was the same skill that had exposed and humiliated his brother at Zetor. To add to the irony, he recalled that he had provoked Yuri at the ČSM meeting for that very same talent.

At that moment, Yuri felt the floor tremble and groan under the weight of heavy footsteps. His widened eyes darted to Josef, who replied in a quiet voice, "He knows how to interrogate. Just follow my lead and tell the truth; never tell him I said that."

A bear of a man emerged from a bedroom, eclipsing the doorway. Squinting with questioning eyes, with the stale scent of alcohol lingering on his breath, and with the manners of a bear, he growled, "You're back late, Josef."

"Good morning, Táta," Josef replied, his tone steady.

The Bear turned his blurry eyes toward Yuri. "Who is this?" Yuri did not feel welcome.

"He's a friend who fixed the motor scooter," Josef said. Yuri noticed his deliberate use of the word "friend." He also observed that Josef responded precisely to his father, giving no more and no less than what was asked. At the mention of the motor scooter, his father's expression darkened, and his breathing became audible.

Josef's father stepped closer, each movement causing the floor to groan under his weight. Towering over Yuri, he studied him intently, like a foreign object. "Why would he do *that*? . . . And Josef, since when have you cared about maintaining the scooter?" All the while, his eyes remained locked on Yuri.

Josef confessed, "I took it to the *fotbol* game. Afterward, I couldn't get it to start. Yuri fixed it."

The Bear slowly digested this information, then belched. "Why did you bring him here?" Yuri felt more unwelcome.

Carefully, Josef replied, "Because if I hadn't, you would have asked, 'Why *didn't* you bring him here?'"

Josef's father focused entirely on Yuri, narrowing his eyes. "Why did you help Josef? Are you a Christian?"

Yuri couldn't believe he was being asked the same question yet again. He answered plainly, "No." And yet, the burden of the denial pressed down on him with an unseen force as he remembered Father Kaleda.

The Bear weighed the crime of Josef using the scooter without permission against the benefit of having it now in good working order. Reckoning still further, his eyes narrowing in the effort, he realized that if not for Josef, he would have broken down.

Still staring at Yuri, Josef's father gruffly muttered, "Hmmm," which Yuri generously interpreted as "Thank you."

Josef recognized the storm had passed when the final growl sounded, "Josef, don't take my scooter without my permission."

A simple meal was offered to Yuri—bread, butter, and coffee. The conversation was sparse. Josef's father said little about himself, and his occupation remained undisclosed, although Yuri had his suspicions.

He couldn't shake the feeling that the man had done bad things. Josef seemed docile in his presence, and despite his gnawing hunger, Yuri found he couldn't eat.

Josef's father dressed neatly and professionally, his clothing plain and unremarkable. As he departed, the scooter groaned under his bulk, its mournful whine fading into the distance.

Yuri relaxed, relieved to be free of this final interview. He felt the loneliness that seemed to define Josef's life. Thoughtlessly, he remarked, "It's funny how everyone left the *fotbol* field without helping you this morning."

Josef stood and gathered the dishes and cups, stacking them in the already crowded sink. Upon returning to the table, he began to wipe it down with a deliberation that felt out of place, given the overall neglect of the housekeeping. Yuri watched, trying to read Josef's mood, but he chose to remain silent.

After washing half the dishes, Josef returned to the table, rested his head in his hands, and answered Yuri's question with careful deliberation.

"People left without helping me because they suspect who my father is. Their suspicions are correct. I'm not allowed to tell you what my father does. You may draw your own conclusions." Josef shifted his hands to the sides of his head, staring blankly at Yuri. "And if you wish to go home as well, I'll understand."

Yuri ignored the invitation to leave and instead blundered into another comment, "Yet Sabrina seems to be on good terms with you."

Josef stood up abruptly once more and continued washing the dishes. The clatter of dishes and the splash of water were more aggressive than before. Some water landed on Yuri.

A rare wind continued to blow outside, causing an elm tree in a nearby small green space to sway. Shadows of young leaves and branches danced across a small spot on the wall and floor where sunlight filtered in. Yuri's attention was drawn to a few photographs illuminated by the light of a younger version of the Bear, a woman who seemed to be his wife, and two young boys. The contrast between the joyful domestic life captured in the photograph and the present reality left a sad impression on Yuri.

Josef finished his work and returned to his seat, now composed but with a few soap suds clinging to his hair. He said a little too loudly, "Yes, she's on good terms with me. My father and Svoboda Sokol have worked together for years. She's been like a sister to me. I wish it were more than that, but she outclasses me. Still, despite knowing this, I can't help but hope—or feel jealous in vain."

He hesitated briefly, irritated by his choice of words—"She outclasses me"—then abruptly shifted the topic, saying, "It's my turn to ask. What was Mr. Sokol talking to you about today?"

"He offered me his support to become a party official," Yuri replied.

Josef stared at Yuri in astonishment, struck by his obliviousness to the favor being offered. His brow furrowed in a battle of emotions. This was the opportunity he had long coveted but had been denied.

He immediately hated Yuri, an outsider and a Bohemian with little investment or loyalty to the party, who seemed indifferent to such a rare and coveted favor. At the same time, he admired and respected Yuri for being chosen for such an esteemed position, for his modesty, and even for condescending to help an enemy. He also considered the practicality of the matter: he had better not offend a future party official.

Seeking further clarification, Josef swallowed and finally asked, "You appear uncertain about this offer. Why?"

Yuri replied, "I'm just uncertain."

Josef continued to stare at Yuri in disbelief. "You don't see it, do you? So this is how you plan to live: as a tiny cog in the Zetor machine?" Josef struggled to leash his emotions. "What is the plan for your little life: earning a little money, marrying a little, unassuming woman, and having a brood of little, ordinary children? Or do you want to make a difference for our country, advancing reforms that will improve everyone's lives? You would be saving the soul of Czechoslovakia."

Yuri responded, "I wish the offer had been given to you." Then, attempting to change the subject, he asked, "Are these pictures of your *Maminka*?"

Josef, unaccustomed to such intimate conversation, felt agitated by the question. Yet, he realized that his mother's story might strengthen his argument. *This is like giving a pill to a dog; you have to wrap it in a piece of meat.* He began to understand the small part he was playing in bringing about a better future for the people and was determined to answer carefully and thoughtfully.

"I barely knew my *Maminka*. After my brother and I were born, things were tight. They struggled for money and food. Those were hungry years. Eventually, she got a work permit in Vienna, Austria. A textile factory. Machine operator. That sort of permit was nearly impossible; my *Táta* pulled strings. Sokol helped. She planned to stay for one year and then return.

"She wrote letters. The work was brutal—heat, noise, back pain.

Same movements, every day. The machines were dangerous—belts, gears, spindles. Everything, everyone, squeezed to the last drop, just to feed the profit.

"My father begged her to come home. She always answered, 'Just a few more weeks.' Then they stopped paying her. No reason she could understand. Later, we found out it was a tactic. Keep the women from quitting.

"She said the factory owner claimed to be a Christian. Said he was following his faith. He preached self-denial and humility. 'Your trials will purify you like gold through fire,' he told them, that sort of thing.

"That's what she wrote in her last letter. Then came the fire—a real fire. No fire exits, no sprinkler systems, no fire-fighting equipment. She was trapped inside along with all the other women."

Josef fell silent, his voice choking with the burden of memory. After a pause, he added with bitterness, "This is why it's worth it. 'The crisis makes men Communists, and the crisis keeps them Communists.' Your inability to decide is because you don't feel the crisis."

Josef slipped into a silent, reflective mood. Sensing it was time to leave, Yuri bid him farewell and stepped out into the sunshine and breeze, beginning the long walk home.

SABRINA

EARLY SPRING, 1972

Intermittent clouds, driven by the wind, alternately bathed Yuri in light and shadow. He could finally breathe again. Josef's words drummed in his head as he walked toward Šimáčkova Street. He felt the weight of the decision before him and welcomed the long walk home. The photograph of Josef's mother and the story of her tragic end pressed upon his mind. He sensed the irony of being accused of being a Christian when stories like hers pushed him further from belief.

Any hope for peace and reflection came to an end. He was upbraided by the same dog that had previously nipped at his heels, now insisting in rapid staccato to "Go home!" The dog trailed Yuri, thinking it would be heard for its many words.

As Yuri approached the house with the flower box and open windows built into its red-tiled roof, a girl peered out, unable to ignore the ruckus.

"Hey there, what are you doing here?" she called to Yuri. Then she addressed the dog, "Dora! Go home!"

Dora became mute and immediately retreated, head down. The mystery of the house with the red Škoda parked in front was resolved. Yuri glanced up, locating the source of the voice, and replied, "Oh, *ahoj.*" Then, to himself: *"Oh boy, I'm not ready for this."*

She said, "Wait for me."

Yuri's eyes dropped to his well-worn jersey and shorts. He examined his hands, still darkened with grease from the scooter repair. As he appraised her home—the finest on the street—he felt ashamed of his slovenly appearance.

His mind wandered to the connection between Mr. Sokol and Josef's father, the Bear. It all quickly became clear. He had heard rumors of torture by the secret police from his father. His heart grew cold. *Why hadn't I seen it sooner? If Josef's father works for the secret police, then her father isn't just a bystander—he's an enforcer of the Party's will. And that almost certainly means torture.* His perception of Sabrina soured.

When the side door opened, and she stepped out, he was more convinced than ever that he was emotionally and mentally unprepared for this meeting. He was also still hungry.

She emerged from the house with a smile and a spring in her step and joined him on the sidewalk. She wore well-tailored jeans and a stylish blouse. Yuri gazed at her with admiration, but his expression betrayed the detritus of stray thoughts.

She tilted her head, looking puzzled. "What?"

Yuri froze at the simplicity of her question. "What do you mean, 'What?'"

Sabrina laughed, amused by his awkwardness. "You looked at me as if we'd never met before," she teased. "And you didn't answer my question. What are you doing here?"

"Ah—yes. I helped Josef repair his scooter. He said his father would want to meet me."

"And you met his father?" she asked, her demeanor sobering. Now, she felt uneasy, having never imagined these two would reconcile.

"Yes. . . . I'm walking home. You can join me if you'd like," he said, wary of her father seeing them together.

Sabrina walked alongside him, breaking the silence first. "I'll walk a little. It was kind of you to help Josef. Most people try to avoid him . . . because of his *táta*. Maybe you've noticed."

"You don't avoid him."

The chess pieces were not moving in her favor. "Noooo," she replied cautiously, puzzled by his cool tone.

"He mentioned that he has known your family for a long time," Yuri continued. "He said you are like a sister to him."

Her response was stiff and brisk: "Did he? Well, I'm glad he thinks so." Then, changing the subject, she added, "My father likes you. He rarely offers patronage to young people, and this is the first time he's done so for an outsider, or a factory worker."

Yuri frowned inwardly, unsure how to interpret her remark. Sokol's stated preference for young people from the working class, outside the city, came to mind, inconsistent with her words. Uncertain how to respond, he allowed the rhythm of his footfalls to answer for him.

Sabrina looked at him, wondering whether he would respond, then persisted, careful not to push too hard. "Usually, when an offer like this is made, it's accepted almost immediately."

Cautiously, and mindful of Sokol's enforcement powers, Yuri replied, "Does your father expect an immediate answer? Since I asked for time to consider his offer, does it come across as being prudent or does it raise suspicion?"

Yuri counted his footsteps, noticing how hers unconsciously fell into rhythm with his. She remained silent but continued to walk beside him. He stole a glance to gauge the effect his words had on her—nothing. He regretted his strong response but let the weight of his words linger. The wind shifted, carrying with it the faint smell of cigarette smoke from her clothes.

Breaking the silence, Yuri asked, "You've grown up in a family of a party official. Would you recommend this life to a friend?"

Sabrina couldn't reply. *A friend? Why does this word sound so sad for the first time in my life?* Her life was constricted by constant scrutiny from higher officials, leaving her family socially isolated. *What is friendship?* With no other experiences to compare it to, she felt at a loss for how to respond. After a moment, embarrassed, she answered quietly, "I don't know . . . I've never had to think about it."

Yuri, who had been so self-conscious just moments ago about his appearance, now perceived a poverty in her life. Beneath her veneer of self-confidence lay emptiness. He contemplated what friendships might be like for someone with a father as a party official. Were people genuine with her, or did they treat her differently because of her father's position, out of fear, or from a desire to curry favor? The thought filled him with profound sadness.

Dora reappeared, quietly trailing behind them. Her toenails scratched a rhythm on the pavement, and her head hung low as she shadowed their steps.

Yuri broke the silence. "Let me tell you a story. Some of my happiest memories with my *Maminka* were the times she read to my sisters and me. Even as teenagers, we enjoyed this family activity. But when I turned fifteen, she became too ill to read to us anymore. After that, without her guiding presence, I began to drift and to get into trouble."

"I learned to drive tractors and moved them around without permission, hiding them where they couldn't be found. I neglected my chores and got into fights with other boys. My *Maminka* was very upset. She would scold me and try to correct my behavior, but I would ignore her.

"Then misfortune struck—I lost her. Her death crushed me, and sorrow followed sorrow. But the grief that clings to me still is this: I never told her I was sorry."

Yuri stole another glance at Sabrina, who walked beside him with her gaze lowered. She listened quietly, as though listening to a sad song, her sympathy evident. He hesitated, measuring the risk of his next words.

"I remembered a story my *Maminka* used to tell me from the Bible—the story of the Prodigal Son," Yuri said. "I don't believe in God. But she did. And she loved that story—about a father running to embrace his son, despite his bad decisions and ruined life. That's what stays with me. It makes me think she would have forgiven me. I don't think I could live in a world without mercy. It comforts me to believe she still would've opened her arms for me."

Dora flopped down on the sidewalk. She had reached her limit.

"I wanted to share that story," Yuri added, "because it has something to do with how I'm thinking about your father's offer. But what about you? Are you happy? Is your family happy?"

He glanced at Sabrina again, but this time her composure faltered. Her eyes reddened, tears pooling as she turned away. Without a word, she slowly walked back toward home.

Yuri stood silently, watching her retreating figure trailed by Dora the Dog. His sorrow deepened—sorrow for both her and himself. He wished to call to her, but hesitated. At that moment, his response to Sokol's offer became clear. She had made it unmistakably plain. Sabrina never turned to look back.

It was mid-afternoon when Yuri entered the apartment. Zofia was the only one home, reading *Lord of the Rings* aloud to Ivana. She didn't acknowledge him, despite his long absence. Yuri had news that he knew would please her, but he decided to keep her in suspense—a subtle retribution for her aloofness.

After finishing a meal of potato soup with sausage and rye, he sat quietly, listening to her read. Poignant, sad, yet comforting memories of his mother reading to him as a child surfaced.

After about half an hour, Zofia set the book down and, in a cool tone, asked, "Don't you have anything better to do than sit and listen to me?" Ivana glanced at Zofia, puzzled by her mercurial mood.

Yuri smiled. "Nope."

Annoyed by his smugness and laconic manner, she pressed, "Aren't you going to tell me where you've been all this time?"

"You didn't ask."

Frustration mounting, Zofia insisted, "Well, I'm asking now."

Yuri finally explained everything—his encounter with Josef, his mother's story, and his decision to refuse Sokol's offer of patronage.

Zofia jumped up, ran over to Yuri, bent over his sitting form, and hugged him.

Ivana giggled at the drama. Still seated, Yuri replied softly, "We will soon find out if I've made a mistake."

FAMILY COUNSEL

LATE SPRING, 1972

"I hope *Táta* will be home for dinner tonight. He's probably forgotten what a warm meal tastes like. I'll make enough for him. Again," Petra complained to Zofia. "All he ever says is, 'I can't tell you what I'm doing. I'm sorry.' Maybe we should hire a spy."

Zofia did not respond.

At the stove, Petra sautéed onions and garlic for the soup, adding dried marjoram and caraway seeds. The fragrance of the onions and garlic filled the apartment, promising comfort and cheer—a promise not to be kept. "May we use the mushrooms you brought home from school yesterday? Where did you find them?" Petra asked.

"Yes," Zofia replied. She avoided any words or gestures that might reveal her connection to Sergei, the source of her mushrooms.

When Yuri arrived, he brought pork schnitzel from the butcher and a few bottles of beer—a rare luxury they reserved for Saturday nights. Petra noticed Zofia glance at Yuri, her expression softening into a genuine but fleeting smile.

The arrival of Václav for dinner was unusual; his presence immediately drew every eye. He wore a boyish expression, as if to say, "What's all the fuss about?" Despite the warmth of his reception, a heaviness settled over the room. Worry etched his face, his movements restrained. His eyes were rimmed with red from sleeplessness.

"Let's eat. We'll talk afterward," he said.

The promise of comfort and cheer remained unfulfilled. Zofia, unusually quiet with an intuitive sense of bad news, pushed food around her plate. Petra attempted, without success, to lighten the mood with questions that went unanswered.

Finally, Václav pushed back from the table, locked his fingers tightly in his lap, and said, "You've all asked me why I'm away so often at night. I will tell you now, but I first need to go back in time. Can you spare a few moments?"

Eager eyes. The sound of breathing.

"About six years ago, your *Maminka* died of TB," he began, pausing to suppress his emotion as he exhaled. "And I blame myself for her death." His voice was choked with emotion. Everyone noticed.

"She went too long without seeing a doctor. When I finally decided to take her, the agriculture commissar on the farm insisted I repair a tractor first. They were unmoved by my plea about her illness. All they cared about were the farm quotas. They had other tractors, but they demanded that this one be fixed. Every decision on the farm went through them."

He paused again, fighting to rein in emotion. They knew the story and wondered why he retold it. He continued, "The repair took time—I had to wait for a part. They wouldn't grant me a permit to leave until the work was done. By the time I got her to the regional hospital, over a month had passed. The doctors informed us she had TB, but it was already too far advanced for treatment."

The children had never witnessed their father speaking so openly and with such raw emotion, even if it was suppressed. They knew the story, but had not considered their father's pain. Attentive silence.

"During the war, I lost men—men who fell following my orders. Their faces haunt me, especially at night. That's why I stay out late—I don't want to remember. You know about my frequent nightmares. Their faces, the weeping families, the burden of their deaths . . . it never leaves. The only small light that made it bearable was knowing we were fighting fascism."

He paused, then exhaled slowly. "But none of that compares to losing your *Maminka*. Her death was personal. It was my fault. And the worst part? The communism I fought for, that we bled for, is worse than the fascism we defeated. I killed her, and they killed her."

The three children sat silently, staring into their father's private purgatory. The shadow of his words settled over them, silencing any hope of comfort. It felt like a confession of the condemned.

"I used to be a loyal communist. I bear the scars to prove it. But after your *Maminka's* death, I don't know what I am anymore. The wound of losing her is deep, but the guilt—my guilt—is unbearable. I can't remain passive. I have a solemn duty to stand against the system that took her from us."

All three children observed their father, the once-proud warrior. They had never heard him speak so much or so openly. As the weight of what he was about to say pressed upon him, he appeared even more aged.

"Last year, a dear friend and fellow soldier wrote to me about a plan. There has been talk of a strike at the Zetor factory. This is another reason keeping me out late." He paused, looking into each of their eyes, allowing the enormity of his revelation to sink in. Zofia began to tremble, and Petra instinctively wrapped her arm around her sister.

"Now you understand why we came to Brno. There were other reasons, but this was the primary one. I couldn't tell you before—the danger was too great. If anything went wrong, you could not be held responsible.

"Why did I agree to help? I do it for your *Maminka*. I do it to find some peace. The chances of something going wrong are high. But even if the worst happens, good will still come from speaking the truth; if not now, then eventually. Still, I am making another sacrifice.

Your suffering presses on me more than I can bear. I don't expect your forgiveness, and I don't deserve it. I hope you understand."

The sun had dropped below the horizon, leaving the dining area draped in shadow. Václav supported his head with his fists, lost in thought. No one turned on the lights. The apartment faded into shadow and darkness. The muted sounds of their neighbors filtered through the walls: the murmur of voices, the blend of news broadcasts and distant music, and the clatter of dishes. These ordinary sounds, once unnoticed, now felt intrusive, mocking the fragile sense of domestic security they clung to.

Zofia wept silently, her normally clear, piercing eyes now vacant and reddened. Václav reached for her hand, but she pulled it away.

Petra rose abruptly and began collecting plates, hoping to distract herself from unwelcome tidings. A knife ominously slipped off a plate, embedding its tip into the wooden floor with a thunk. Petra yanked it out, the force of her gesture leaving no doubt how she felt.

Václav continued. "Petra, stop a moment." She reluctantly returned. "Just listen. I've made plans—or tried to. The Krčméry family in Třeboň, whose books Zofia copied, has offered to shelter you girls. I've been working on getting the permits. I'm also trying to get one for Yuri, though I don't think you'll need it.

"The problem is, I can't go through official channels. The Internal Travel Permit application covers only things like work, family visits, or medical reasons. There's no option for 'protection of dissidents' children.' Worse, if I filed a permit, it would bring attention I can't afford. It would unravel everything we've tried to keep hidden.

"I asked a friend to forge the permits, but it's taking longer than expected. Time has run out. Yuri, your run-in with the officials at Zetor gave the strike momentum, but it also put me in the spotlight and moved the schedule forward. The strike is set for Wednesday. It's a moving train that I can no longer stop."

Turning to Yuri, Václav said, "I kept you out of the whisper networks at work for a reason. You may have noticed the slowdowns at work over the past few months. They weren't accidents. They were tests. Ways to build trust, to measure resolve. I'll put you into the picture soon. But right now, we have to stay focused on what's ahead."

"The strike begins Wednesday afternoon. And whether you meant to or not, Yuri, the moment you repaired that tractor months ago, you touched a sensitive spot. The workers saw it. They remembered. You've become something of a symbol to them now. A name they rally around."

Václav spread a significant sum of cash on the table. "The

consequences of the strike are uncertain, as are the permit forgeries. Life may become difficult for a time. This money should cover household expenses for over a month. I've withdrawn all of our savings because there's a chance they'll freeze our account. So, no more beer for a while. Keep this money well hidden.

"There's a good chance I'll be arrested. Yuri, they may take you in, too, just because of your connection to me. If that happens, I expect they'll release you quickly, I hope. You weren't part of the planning. Zetor may shut down for a time, but when the machines start up again, I believe they'll bring you back, with the others."

I expect? thought Yuri.

Turning to the girls, Václav said, "Zofia, Petra, you need to be ready for what may come at school. Expulsion is possible. Likely, even. They'll be watching the house, watching you. For a while, everything we do will feel like it's under glass.

"Zofia, Petra, when the permits arrive, go to Třeboň at once. The Krčméry family will take you in. They will vouch for you, shelter you, and keep you safe. While there, keep a low profile. No more copying banned books. Stay away from the local authorities. Work hard. Make yourselves useful in every way you can. If someone grows suspicious, your diligence might be enough to make them look the other way.

"I have a friend—an official—who knows your situation. He's willing to silence suspicions or butter a few palms if it comes to that. If the permits arrive after the strike, leave at night. Less chance of being seen. And if they don't arrive at all. . . . Then I don't know. Yuri, you'll have to find a way. But I believe they'll come. And when they do, you'll have a two-week window, one-way passage, Třeboň only."

Petra shook her head, unable to believe what she heard. Despite the gravity of the situation, the thought of returning to her old home lifted her spirits. Zofia quietly wept.

Resigned, Yuri ventured a comment, "*Táta* . . . are you sure?" Václav replied, "It's too late. Even if I stand still, it changes nothing. As I said, it's a train already in motion."

STRIKE

LATE SPRING, 1972

The overnight rain clouds cleared in the early morning. The sun shone bright, promising a cheery day. Yuri and his father waited on the platform for the next tram to the Zetor Tractor factory. Václav had risen very early to meet with strike agitators and returned home to accompany Yuri, cherishing the brief time they had together. He tried to say goodbye to his daughters, but their door remained shut and silent.

As they waited at the tram stop, Václav said, "I think the years we worked together in the mechanics workshop in Třeboň are my happiest. Yuri, you're a good mechanic."

The comment was not something his father would normally say. He felt a chill. The routine morning stood in stark contrast to the gathering storm.

"I believe most will fall in line when the time comes," Václav said. "Do as you wish, but the tide of workers may be stronger than your will. Trust me. Unfortunately for you, as I've said before, most workers see you as their champion. It'll be difficult to resist joining the resistance. I haven't even spoken to you about the reasons why we're striking. I'm sorry, I couldn't. You'll know soon enough."

Yuri glanced at his father, admiring his manly virtue and noting his childlike warmth and cheerfulness. Although he must have had countless concerns in leading the strike, he couldn't remember when he had seen his father so much at peace. Yuri studied him closely, searching for any hint of madness in his decision to risk everything on a high-stakes venture destined to fail.

Yuri had not yet decided whether to join the strike. However, the thought of standing apart and enduring the shame of not standing alongside his father was inconceivable.

Yuri asked, "When will the girls' travel permits be ready? I would feel much better knowing they are secure."

"So would I," Václav replied. "I hope it's soon. They told me it takes time to obtain an authentic blank form. It's costly—both in time and money. We have to wait. The man I hired is good."

"Remember what I told you. Don't forget," Václav continued. "Someone you don't know, but who knows you, will slip you a note. It'll be encoded. You have the key to decode it. The message will tell you when and where to make the handoff. Bring a newspaper to hide the travel permits. You'll get instructions on where to exit. Quickly. Quietly. Here. Take this envelope. In it you'll find 1,500 crowns. Keep it on you. You may need it."

The familiar tram arrived, and they boarded in silence. Soon, they reached Zetor on a morning like any other. Václav lingered, his steps slow and deliberate, stalling. Another tram approached, and Miloslav disembarked. He joined Václav, and the two men walked together slowly, their conversation muted. Miloslav glanced at Yuri with a broad, genuine smile, a look that conveyed respect. As they continued their slow walk, they gathered other workers and casually exchanged final instructions.

With a view of what lay ahead, Václav stopped and rested his hand firmly on Yuri's shoulder. Meeting his son's gaze, he said, "I love you, son."

Yuri followed them into the plant. Entering the familiar surroundings felt like a leap into the unknown. The plan unfolded seamlessly. So far. For now, they maintained the upper hand.

Workers settled into their stations, starting promptly at 6:00 AM. The assembly line moved tractors through its slow, continuous rhythm. The unceasing sounds of production filled the air: the low-frequency hum of factory equipment, the crackle and pop of welding, the pounding of hammers, and staccato bursts from pneumatic tools. Overseeing it all, unwary managers and Party officials observed and listened, confident that all would continue unchanged, just as it always had under their capable leadership, and that the State's five-year productivity goals would be met without disruption.

Yuri frequently glanced at the clock, counting the minutes to the agreed-upon time when everything would change.

At 1:13 PM, time stood still. The relentless, roaring symphony of the factory gradually faded into silence. Conveyor belts slowed to a halt. Forklifts were parked. Tools were set down. The hum of electricity, the final refrain of sound, clicked off. The silence left a ringing in the ears. Then, the echo of footsteps emerged, growing louder.

Yuri examined the workers' expressions as they filed out, uncertain of what to expect. They moved with courage and a shared belief in the principles of the strike. Older workers nearing retirement and more risk-averse stayed inside, bearing the shame of separation.

How strange to see these workers stand together in solidarity. Real solidarity—against the State. United in something they believe in. But the Party won't back down. If tractor production stops, steel will follow, then coal, then the railways. They won't let that happen. This strike is hopeless. Everyone is walking out. Following Táta. Do they understand what they're walking into?

As foretold, Yuri felt drawn into the current, his reluctance melting away. When he rose and joined the throng, he was greeted cheerfully. Fellow workers, finally freed from months of suppressed admiration for Yuri's past courage, welcomed him with open enthusiasm. These shared moments among the workers were exhilarating, as if, for the first time in their lives, they could finally speak and walk in the truth.

The group gathered in an empty overflow parking lot just north of the main entrance, a space typically reserved for finished tractors. From seemingly nowhere, banners emerged, unfurled with slogans reflecting the workers' demands. Members of the press arrived as scheduled— neither too early to risk exposure nor too late to capture the moment. Miloslav stepped forward to engage with the news media, conducting interviews.

Václav claimed the central position, climbed a step ladder with a loudspeaker in hand, and waited. A hush settled over the workers as Václav took his place. The atmosphere was thick with an uneasy calm. Yuri scanned the faces of the men around him—some etched with fear, others hardened with joyful resolve, ready for the fight ahead.

Managers, union representatives, and others not aligned with the strike emerged from the front entrance, squinting against the bright sun. Under its intense glare, they appeared pallid and less threatening, their authority washed out. Some clutched cups of coffee, attempting to project an air of control. Others stood uneasily, brows furrowed, lips firmly set, anticipating a swift and severe resolution. The *stranící* followed, with Svoboda Sokol at the forefront, a loudspeaker in hand. This was the cue Václav had been waiting for.

Raising his loudspeaker, Václav began to speak. "Fellow workers, we stand united for a safe workplace and a voice in decisions on the factory floor. We stand in solidarity with one another and with the Pokorný family. Six months ago, this husband and father, a respected worker, lost an arm to the industrial press. Fatigued by an unreasonable and increased workload, he came too close to danger. Since then, his family has suffered. His children have been pulled out of school to help support their household . . ."

Sokol raised his loudspeaker and cut in, "Pokorný lost his arm because he was drunk . . ."

The factory workers grumbled with anger.

Václav ignored the provocation and pressed on. ". . . And we stand in solidarity against the unjust punishment imposed on my son and others like him who acted in the best interests of Zetor. My son was wrongly accused of negligence for a problem he did not cause. He repaired an issue that was someone else's responsibility. If it were investigated, it may have been sabotage. He was punished for this. No apology was offered. You have prioritized ideological purity over merit.

"To the management of Zetor, we appeal to your sense of reason and justice: our demands serve the interests of both the factory and the socialist state. A safer workplace and a satisfied workforce will lead to higher-quality tractors. Improved tractors will strengthen Zetor as a company and benefit the farmers in the field, and enhance the State's prestige. Our western competitors . . .”

Sokol's grating, raspy voice broke through once again, amplified by the loudspeaker's squealing feedback. "This is your final warning. Return to your stations immediately. Dvořák, stick to what you do best—building tractors—and leave the decisions on how to build them to us. *We* decide how everyone works according to their ability and receives according to their needs." His attempt at lofty rhetoric ended abruptly in a fit of coughing.

The crowd grumbled even louder. Yuri stepped forward, positioning himself next to his father. As Václav's chances of success dwindled, Yuri's respect for him increased.

"Sokol, the men standing with me today, taking such a risk, bear witness that your leadership is found wanting. Step aside. You do not serve the interests of the workers as you claim. From now on, we will negotiate only with the director and the deputy directors."

Sokol rasped into his loudspeaker, "Abandon hope, Dvořák. By raising this rabble against the State, you condemn yourself. You are the one who divides, not us. Do you truly believe your petty grievances outweigh the welfare of the state? You dare to criticize our leadership and make us the enemy? You are the enemy. Your illegal strike is proof enough. You are a cancer, a traitor to the very people you pretend to defend. Your arrogance will only lead to misery and suffering for your workers. This is your final warning—disband now, or there will be no mercy."

He stood with squared shoulders, his jaw clenched, and his arms folded to project dominance. However, a careful observer would have noticed his knees shaking.

Václav turned to the workers, many of whom now shifted nervously, unsettled by Sokol's last volley of words. "Take heart, men. 'Faithless is he who says farewell when the road darkens.' Remember Jan Hus, who stood against corruption and tyranny in his time. Let us honor his memory by remaining steadfast, no matter the cost."

Turning back to Sokol, Václav said, "I fought alongside men who sacrificed their lives on the Eastern Front to free our country from Nazi occupation. I am no traitor. We were promised a bright future under communism, but instead, we've been given something worse by people like you. I didn't believe it at the time, but now I do. The State robbed me of my farm. The State made demands on my family years ago; I consented under compulsion, and now, as a result, my wife is dead and buried. She correctly spoke of people like you: 'You are a waterless spring and a cloud without rain driven along by a storm.'"

Yuri watched in disbelief. Was this man, standing so boldly, truly his father? At this moment, Yuri saw his father's strength as never before. Yet he also feared that he had gone too far. *Well, now he's done it. All these years, the truth has lain dormant. I hope Maminka is proud of him for this.*

The sharp wail of sirens shattered the tension. Riot police arrived, lights flashing as they poured out of their vehicles, batons and shields in hand, tear gas canisters hanging from their belts. They moved swiftly to form a blockade, surrounding the strikers and preventing them from spilling into the neighboring areas or regrouping elsewhere.

Václav turned to the workers, raising his voice above the commotion. "Courage, men. No violence. Hold fast. What we are doing does not require violence. Our peaceful resistance speaks truth more powerfully than any weapon. It will be remembered. Stand your ground, let them make the next move."

Then, facing the gathering crowd of onlookers, he called out, "Citizens of Brno, stand with us in solidarity. Our struggle is not ours alone, but for all of you who believe in . . ."

Three canisters of tear gas were lobbed into the group of workers. Anticipating this, the men covered their faces with wet rags and, with gloved hands, picked up the canisters to cast them aside. Yet, the thick, acrid cloud was nearly overwhelming. One worker, defying orders, threw a canister back at the police. The provocation triggered a baton charge. As instructed, the men dropped to their knees en masse, linking arms in passive resistance, a strategy that garnered sympathy from the growing crowd. Bodies braced for impact. Despite injuries and bloodshed as shields crashed into the first row of strikers, the line held. Eventually, the police were ordered to retreat, and a tense stand-off ensued.

As second-shift workers arrived, they were prevented from joining the strike. More onlookers gathered, many arriving by tram, creating a spectacle that became intolerable for the Ministry of the Interior. Chaos ensued; voices from the crowd cheered on the workers. Orders for mass arrests were issued. Police vans forced their way through the crowd, and officers handcuffed protesters with excessive force, pushing them into the vehicles.

Three police officers approached Václav. In a passionate attempt to protect his father, Yuri overpowered them, grabbing a baton raised to strike, wrenching it from the officer's grip, and wielding it to shield his father. A fourth officer blindsided Yuri, subduing him with force.

As Yuri, now bleeding, and his father were led toward a police van, Yuri scanned the crowd of onlookers. He spotted Zofia and Petra, their tear-streaked faces shouting unheard words. He also noticed Sabrina, standing frozen, staring in disbelief with her arms tightly folded despite the warm spring weather.

Yuri walked beside his father, hands cuffed behind his back. As long as he stayed with his captain, his courage held strong. But then an order came, and Václav—along with Miloslav—was taken away in a separate police vehicle. Yuri's heart sank as he locked eyes with his father. He wondered, filled with dread, if he would ever see him again. An abyss opened before him as the van doors slammed shut. He cried out for his father, wrenching himself away from his captors. The struggle was brief; he fell into darkness.

INTERROGATION

LATE SPRING, 1972

Yuri slowly recovered consciousness as the police van roughly navigated the streets of Brno. Headache. Dizziness. Pain from blows to the head. He had difficulty remembering anything. His head rested in someone's lap. Yuri attempted to sit up, but a friend gently urged him to lie back down, holding him securely to prevent his body from rolling as the van careened through the streets.

The police van arrived at the rear of a drab concrete building with small, reinforced windows, concealed from public view. There were no signs. As he stepped out of the van, he saw the blood-soaked rag that had been beneath his head. Although they were tightly escorted, Yuri's friends were permitted to help him walk. With mental effort, he tried to remember. *Why am I here? Where's my Táta? What will happen to Zofia and . . . what's her name? . . . Petra?*

The prisoners were coerced with harsh language and physical intimidation to hurry. The police found the task of booking the prisoners distasteful. After surrendering personal information and being stripped of their clothes and possessions, they were all issued ill-fitting prison attire, each marked with an identification number. Yuri resigned himself to never seeing the money his father gave him again.

Yuri was separated from the others and led through a maze of narrow, dimly lit hallways lined with closed doors. He felt nauseous. He was hungry. His ears were ringing. He began to recall something about the strike.

Eventually, the prison warden found a detention cell, unlocked the door, and thrust him inside. The door slammed shut behind him with a heavy thud, leaving him in an oppressive space. Silence swallowed the sounds of the warden's retreating footsteps.

Bewildered by the furious, chaotic sequence of events, Yuri dropped to his knees and sat on the ground. He realized he was not alone. Confused, he looked up at a fellow cellmate and murmured, more to himself, "What did I do?"

A voice answered waspishly, "That's what they always say: 'What did I do?' Or 'What for?' Or 'Why me?' But you know. Stop fooling yourself. You went against the organs of the State, and now you're arrested, and you say, 'What did I do?' You'd better have something else to say besides 'What did I do?' when they come to interrogate you."

Yuri, still recovering from the concussion, crawled to the toilet and vomited. He then crept back to a corner, leaned against the wall, thought for a moment of his unfriendly roommate, slumped onto the cold concrete floor, and fell asleep.

Yuri awoke and drank the brown liquid hungrily from the sink faucet. The bare light bulb above was always on, casting a harsh glare. The barred windows revealed it was night. He was alone. He considered lying on the bunk, but it was too late. A guard unlocked the door. Yuri jerked to attention. Still feeble, vulnerable, and hungry, with an aching head, Yuri hoped for food. Instead, he was taken forcefully from his cell.

More hallways. More doors. No signs, just numbers. Yuri was taken to a room with a heavy metal table and two chairs. Yuri's chair was bolted to the floor. The warden cuffed his wrists to the table and shackled his ankles to the ground.

More waiting. Yuri began to doze. A strikingly beautiful, well-dressed woman entered the room and sat opposite Yuri. She spoke to him in a friendly, almost apologetic, tone for "all the inconvenience we have caused you." She removed her beret, unpinned her hair, and let it fall. "You've had a terrible blow to your head. After our chat, we must give you medical attention and a comfortable place to rest and recover." She lazily discussed the weather and everything she looked forward to as the season warmed: cycling, canoeing. "Have you ever canoed near Český Krumlov? It's such a beautiful place, near where you once lived." She took off her blazer and scarf. She mentioned the strike and assured Yuri that everything would be okay, suggesting there had probably been a mistake in communication. Yuri began to relax.

She took off her shoes, removed the bow tie from her neck, and began unbuttoning her blouse. Yuri felt confused. Picnicking. Hiking. Shopping. She took off her blouse and bra, then sat next to him on the table with a coy smile. She produced a key to unlock the handcuffs and placed it on the table. And there she sat. Yuri looked down, flushed and trembling, short of breath.

"I'd like to show you my favorite places for canoeing someday," the beautiful woman said, her voice gentle and inviting. "There are secluded spots; truly lovely places to . . . well, we can talk about that later."

He continued to tremble, fighting the urge to look at her. He glanced up, searching her face for any trace of guile. She was indeed beautiful. Her expression revealed a questioning innocence and sincerity that were disarming, confusing, and tempting for him. He dropped his gaze again, grinding his teeth as he often did in dreams of free-falling through endless space.

Her tone shifted slightly, taking on a curious, probing edge. "Tell me about your father. . . . And Miloslav. . . . Surely you must have known about the planning for the strike."

"I don't know," Yuri replied repeatedly. Part of him almost

wished he had something to confess to end the witchery. However, another part was tempted to fabricate lies to prolong her solicitation for information. And so it continued.

Finally, she stood up from the table, casually took a seat in the chair opposite Yuri, reached into her handbag, and pulled out a revolver. She slammed it on the table, the barrel aimed at Yuri, and shouted furiously, "Talk! We know you took part in organizing the strike. We know you betrayed your comrades."

Yuri was completely bewildered. A snake had emerged from an alluring flower. Fear coiled inside his chest, working itself into his throat. He replied with a broken voice, "What do you want me to talk about?"

"You're wasting my time. You know what to talk about, you idiot!"

"There was a strike . . . "

"'There was a strike.'" She interrupted with a shrill, almost demonic, mocking voice, eyes blazing, "Of course, there was a strike! Tell me everything, or I'll put a slug into your skull!"

". . . and at the appointed time, I walked out with everyone else. That's all."

She fired off a barrage of questions: "Did you know your father was planning a strike? Who did your father know? Is there a coalition of factories planning the same thing? What part did you play in the organization?"

Yuri denied any knowledge. The woman picked up the revolver and examined it, her eyes wild and menacing. She would hold it to his head while asking questions. Shaking with fear, Yuri was certain he was going to die. The interview continued.

She changed her tone again, speaking in a sweet and friendly manner. She placed the revolver back on the table and began putting on her clothing, smiling at him seductively all the while. "Does my bow tie look straight? Oh, I'm sorry. You're acting like you don't care," she said petulantly.

Sitting again on the table beside Yuri, she spoke like a mother correcting a wayward son: "Here, will you help me with this last button behind my neck? . . . Oh, I'm so sorry, I forgot about your shackles." She giggled. "Yuri Dvořák, I hope you change your mind about cooperating with us. Your outcome has already been decided; we have the proof. If you resist, you'll die here in prison. If you confess, they'll send you to a nice prison camp where you'll enjoy fresh air, sunlight, and food. I hope very soon this matter can be resolved."

She lied. The uranium mining prison camps in the Jáchymov

region had stopped using forced labor for ten years, but few people knew this. "I wish I could have gotten to know you better. Maybe we'll meet again, soon," she said with an enticing smile. She picked up her pistol and handcuff keys, placed them in her purse, and then departed.

Eventually, a guard entered with a smirk, unshackled Yuri, and yanked him up, leading him down another maze of hallways. His hope for unconsciousness grew stronger with each dragging step. They entered a room filled with bright light and a soft sofa. "Sit!" the guard commanded. Yuri immediately obeyed, lying his head back to sleep. He was kicked hard. "No sleeping!"

Yuri realized standing would be preferable to enduring the sofa's comfort without permission to sleep. "May I stand?" He inferred the answer after another sharp kick.

Four days later. No sleep. Severely bruised shins. A one-third kilogram of bread and one glass of water per day. The guards changed every four hours. They all did their job well. Yuri deteriorated.

On the fifth day, a guard received instructions to transport Yuri to another interrogation room. His prison clothes, once tight-fitting, now sagged. He attempted to stand but immediately fell, overcome by dizziness. The guard roughly and unnecessarily placed him in an escort hold, and they continued walking.

Yuri saw something on the hallway floor—his dog, Thor, lying in a pool of blood and being eaten by buzzards. The birds turned their reddened eyes on Yuri, picked up Thor, and flew away. He would have collapsed if not for the guard's hold. Yuri cried out, "Thor!" He was trapped in a nightmare, his voice muted when he tried to cry out.

They walked past, and the vision of Thor's blood on the floor vanished. He heard Petra's voice whispering in his ears, insisting that he needed to come home. This, too, faded. He saw his father and two sisters at an intersection in the hallway, their backs to him as they walked away. His father turned to look at him, expressing disappointment and reproach—another hallucination.

He found himself locked in another interrogation room with a glass door. The hallucinations persisted. The chair on the opposite side of the table started to move. He fought to maintain his grip on reality.

No guard. He could sleep.

Suddenly, he heard a woman screaming in the next room, followed by prolonged weeping. *This is not a hallucination!* The screaming continued. Yuri looked through the glass door and saw Petra pass by, her head down. He struggled to understand what was real. He thought Petra was suffering because of him. *What did I do? I did this to her.*

The strain was becoming unbearable. A profound hopelessness overwhelmed him.

Petra appeared before him in a hallucination, accusing him of her beatings, and then vanished. More screaming, more weeping. The real and the illusory swirled in his mind.

The door opened and closed. A large man entered and sat opposite Yuri. Sleep deprivation heightened every stimulus. Yuri jerked at his entry, straining against his shackles and drawing blood.

He tried to focus on the large man, his eyes wild with fear; the man looked familiar.

"You're looking a little thin since the last time I saw you. You must not have enough gratitude for our food, eh?" the man mocked slowly. "I remember you. You were in my home once. Of course! You're the Christian. Where is your God now? God doesn't care for little rabbits like you. Do you think that your God can deliver you from me, little rabbit?"

More screams echoed from the room next door. Yuri fought to piece together the fragments of memory.

"If you cooperate, your sister walks free. If you refuse, we'll lock her up with men who are, let's say, not shining examples of moral virtue," he said, laughing, proud of his clever understatement.

Yuri trembled, rocking back and forth in his seat, arms crossing his chest. He saw a vision of his mother, with her back turned toward him. She turned and glanced at him with an expression of bitterness and disappointment. "Why?" was all she said.

Yuri began beating his head with his fists.

"Are you ready to tell me who your father was working with? Who are the other leaders and strike organizers? We know that you know. We have proof."

"I only . . . knew about my father."

The Bear slammed his fist on the table and leaned over Yuri, shouting inches from his face. His breath had a foul odor. Yuri jerked violently again. More blood.

"Are you telling me that you are the son of one of the strike organizers, and that's all you know? You moved from Třeboň to Brno to organize a strike. You were likely one of the organizers. Don't tell me you knew nothing, you idiot!"

"I didn't even know about the strike. . . ."

"Liar! We will bleed you drop by drop. I'll send Vlasta, the man-slayer, to you again. She may be more promiscuous this time . . . with her *bullets*. We know your father was a Western agent."

Yuri's mind spun with confusion. He had been unaware of his

father's war experiences—perhaps there were other things he didn't know. He shook violently.

The Bear declared that Yuri's physical altercation with the police, in defense of his father, was sufficient to lock him away for years. More questions were hurled at Yuri. The Bear inquired about connections to dissident groups, foreign actors, and other organizations. Adhering to prescribed methods of interrogation, he left no signs of physical abuse. Any allegations of torture could be easily denied. However, the scars of torture were indelibly etched on his soul.

"Please send my sister home," Yuri pleaded, ready to confess anything, even if it wasn't true. Yet, his mind was too far gone even to fabricate a lie.

Yuri was led to a two-by-three-meter prison cell when the session ended. Inside, there was a single narrow bed, a stool, and a table, all bolted to the floor. Another person was already in this cell, awakened by the commotion. Yuri was shoved inside, and he collapsed immediately onto the floor, sinking into a deep, dreamless coma.

Yuri drifted in and out of consciousness. When he finally came to, he found himself on a bed, unable to lift his head.

"Welcome back to the land of the living," a kind voice said. Yuri noticed another prisoner sitting near him, and shrank back. The other prisoner was smiling. It was evening. "You've slept well—nearly 20 hours. You need to eat. No, stay in bed. It's yours until you've recovered. My name is Alyosha."

Alyosha brought him food. "Eat slowly. Small portions. Don't protest. Trust me. You will need your strength. This is just the beginning."

ZOFIA

LATE SUMMER, 1972

Yuri was easily startled by the occasional cough or sneeze. He tried to conceal these reactions, knowing they might appear strange. He had difficulty concentrating, attempting to remember where he was in Brno as the tram presented rapidly changing views. Having been imprisoned for three months, the passing scenes of medieval and Baroque buildings, squares and plazas, parks, and green spaces evoked mixed emotions in him, like the thrill and terror a child would experience being tossed into the air.

On the one hand, the passing scenes distracted him from terrible memories. On the other hand, the press of people sitting and standing around him, the pulsing sensations of light and shadow, and the constant starting and stopping caused sensory overload, heightening his anxiety. Passengers cast wary glances at the unshaven figure among them. His hollow eyes and stiff, unnatural movements set them on edge. They kept their distance as if he were a dangerous animal.

The tram approached the Líšeňská rokle, the ravine where he had accumulated so many memories. However, Yuri almost missed his stop. He snapped upright as the tram slowed and disembarked jerkily through open doors. The passengers were relieved to see this human oddity go. He descended the stairs, found a park bench, and sat for a while, hoping to recover from the ride and rest in the solitude. His heartbeat gradually slowed. He rocked back and forth, pressing his hands against the seat.

A stranger sitting nearby rose and walked over to Yuri, discreetly handing him a tightly folded wad of paper before passing on. Yuri didn't have enough time to assess whether he was in danger from this passing stranger; it all happened too quickly. The wad remained hidden in his hand as he struggled to understand what it was. He wanted to remember, but could not. He knew better than to open it there.

He watched as an elderly woman moved among the trees separating the *paneláky* from the ravine, her arms loaded with sunflowers, considered a weed by most but a touch of beauty and joy for her lonely apartment. Yuri tried to hold onto a single thought: a normal life, a room with a table, a simple jar of flowers sitting on the table. He remembered the spring flowers his sisters had used to brighten their dying mother's bedroom. The flowers faded, the petals fell, and his mother slipped away forever. Yuri rocked back and forth on his seat, weeping. *Maminka, I'm really sorry for what I did.*

Trams came and went, their passage echoing like the wind among the apartments. He continued to sit, wondering why he was reluctant to return home, struggling to remember. Thoughts of Alyosha flooded his mind, filling him with guilt for leaving his friend behind, imprisoned. *Alyosha the madman, who forgave the men who broke him and still spoke of some golden future. . . . My friend, Alyosha. He gave up his food when I was starving. He kept me alive when I wanted to die. Again and again, he brought me back.*

His mind drifted to Sabrina, recalling how she had often stolen her way into his dreams during his imprisonment. The life he once knew was lost, as was the future he had dared to hope for.

Yuri went over the strange circumstances of his release. He alone had been discharged. Reaching into his pocket, he felt the envelope they'd given him—discharge papers, so he thought. When he opened it, he was surprised to find all the money his father had given him.

He was anxious to see his sisters. Yet Yuri rocked slightly in his seat, remaining planted, fear constricting his chest. He worried that his return might bring them trouble. He feared the unblinking eyes of surveillance, felt ashamed of his shabby appearance, and carried the weight of regret for the sorrow he had caused them. *Why didn't I stay home that day? I could have called in sick. I thought it might be an adventure. I didn't think about Petra. Or Zofia. I was proud when* Táta *said I had become a kind of hero for the workers. I just wanted to be near him.*

And then it struck him. *Petra was in the prison!* The memory burst into clarity. *I heard her screams. I saw her walk by the glass door. That wasn't a hallucination.*

Yuri sprang to his feet and began walking quickly toward the apartment. He deftly slipped the wad of paper into his pocket. Skirting the edge of a makeshift soccer field and passing like a scarecrow past the bright, athletic youth, he hoped not to be recognized. The happy spring days of *fotbal* felt so distant.

Inside the apartment building, Yuri encountered Ivana in the hallway. "Why do I never see Miss Zofia? Do you know where she is?" she asked hastily. Her eyes narrowed as she scrutinized Yuri more closely in the dim light, then turned and ran off before he could respond.

Yuri unlocked the apartment door and stepped inside. Petra was gathering tomatoes into her apron from the small balcony garden when she heard the door open. She peered inside towards the hall door, not expecting anyone to enter. Their eyes met, and she froze. Yuri studied her face—something in her expression was off. He dismissed the lack of warmth as a reaction to his wild appearance.

"You're here! Are you alright?" Yuri cried out.

In a controlled manner, she delivered the tomatoes to the sink, then approached him cautiously, studying him with an expression of fear and disbelief, her eyes wide. She was off-balance by his sudden arrival and strange question.

"Well, sort of. You sound like something terrible happened."

"It *was* terrible," Yuri replied. "Weren't you taken into custody and tortured? I saw you; I heard your screams."

Petra slowly shook her head, her eyes fixed on Yuri. Now, she was truly worried about his behavior. "No, nothing like that. I was summoned for some procedural nonsense. I signed a paper, and they told me to walk across the hall with my head down. They threatened me severely if I raised it. I did as they asked—twice, for reasons I don't understand. I heard screaming, too, but it wasn't me. Then they released me."

For a moment, Yuri struggled to remember and comprehend, trying to reconcile her account with his own. He exhaled, his shoulders sagging. It was all a deception. He fell to his knees, visibly relieved by the news.

"Oh, Yuri!" was all Petra could manage as her heart wrenched at the sight of him. She knelt, then gently and carefully embraced him. He followed her lead, and together they sobbed, though his cries were deeper and longer. Teardrops appeared on the back of her garment. She said as he wept, "What happened to you in there?"

They sat on the ground together in silence, both unfamiliar with each other's presence and uncertain of what to say—time had altered them both. Petra's expression held an embarrassed reserve. Yuri's face had thinned; all expression had been wrung out of it. His clothes hung loosely. His voice was thin. He stared out the window without focus, through the tomato vines, into the ravine.

He said, "I can't tell you what happened. I was tortured multiple times—psychological torture. I often hallucinated. I couldn't distinguish reality from illusion. For months, I thought you and Zofia were being tortured in prison. By the way, have you heard from *Táta?*"

Petra replied, "I was going to ask you the same."

The subject was too painful to discuss further. The wave of sorrow he felt at his father's absence was nearly suffocating. More time passed.

Yuri glanced at Petra, puzzled by her uncharacteristically quiet behavior. *Maybe it's not me.*

Petra broke the silence and began, "Zofia and I were both summoned by the school authorities. Representatives of the State Security Police were present. They informed us that we were expelled and provided the reasons. I don't need to explain why. They made us sign a document acknowledging the expulsion. And that was it."

Yuri nodded but remained silent, preparing himself for more bad news. His eyes examined Petra's face. She appeared worn down by worry, thinner than he recalled, and her appearance seemed neglected. There was more; her eyes concealed something.

Petra stood up and began searching the kitchen. She returned with what little she could find, or to make it appear so: some bread, leftover sausage, and a few tomatoes. "We don't have much food," she admitted, feeling embarrassed. "We're barely getting by. Remember the garden you helped me with? The tomatoes are from there—our little garden. I'm scared, Yuri."

Yuri accepted the food and ate wolfishly. As he ate, he regained some faculty of his mind, little by little. Petra interrupted his singular focus on eating, "What happened to you in there?"

The memories suffocated Yuri. He stopped chewing, shut his eyes, and shook his head. He was unable to speak, knowing that voicing memories would reawaken the ghosts. Finally, he swallowed.

"Please, not now. Some other time. . . . Where is Zofia?"

"She's fine. She's . . . with a friend," Petra replied, her voice stiff and her composure faltering. Yuri looked down and kept eating.

After a moment, he glanced at her, then stood up from his meal and began to pace the room, agitated and lost in thought. He moved to the window, gazing out through the dying, yellowing tomato vines toward the ravine below, his eyes searching as if hoping to catch a glimpse of Zofia. He stopped and glanced again at Petra with fierce eyes.

"Did she say when she would be back?"

"Probably later tonight."

"Probably?" Yuri's voice was strained with rising anxiety. "What friend would she be with at this hour? It's unusual for her to be out so late. She's usually home reading or doing homework. Even Ivana asked about her in the hallway. Does Zofia do this regularly?" Yuri's voice choked with concern. He shook with uncontrollable emotion.

He turned and glanced at Petra, her hands tightly clasped in her lap. She looked up at him, blinking nervously. Yuri had changed—his agitation was unfamiliar to her, and his eyes burned with a wild, untamed intensity. She remained silent.

"*Táta* left you just a little more than a month's wages. How are you managing to pay for food and rent? I've been away for over three months." Yuri's agitation and voice were rising.

Petra rubbed her temples, her composure crumbling. "Zofia is out with Sergei… He gives her money. We needed that money!"

Yuri's voice grew louder and more urgent. "Where is Zofia? I mean, *where* is she?"

Tears streamed down Petra's face. "I don't know!" she cried. "Sergei gets on the tram at the Krásného stop. What are you going to do? You can't go there!" She stood abruptly, stepping close to Yuri, her voice lowering to a frantic whisper, "What are you going to do? They're watching us; they're probably listening to our talk right now."

"Then stop talking." Yuri stormed into the girls' bedroom, his movements wild as he began tearing through Zofia's belongings. Petra stood frozen in the doorway, watching the chaos unfold. He rifled through desk drawers, scattering slips of paper and tossing notebooks and books onto the floor. Clothes were pulled from their places and piled on the floor. Finally, he found an envelope with Sergei's address tucked into a sweater pocket. He grabbed a city map and stormed out of the apartment. Petra remained mute and helpless, unable to stop him from his madness.

Outside, Yuri found the same park bench and collapsed onto it, breathing heavily. With unsteady hands, he opened the map, studied it, and pinpointed the address. He was consumed by rage, a primal desire for retribution and rescue. *This is right what I must do*, he breathed to himself, even as he knew his wrath was spiraling out of control. He had to save his sister; he feared he might kill Sergei.

His resolve became unyielding, though his body felt weakened from days of near-starvation. The devil was gaining the upper hand.

He stepped off the tram at the Krásného stop, stumbling over a hardwood stick about half a meter long. He picked it up, gripping it tightly as he unfolded his map, studied it again by lamplight, and scanned the area. His search led him to a blockhouse, like every other blockhouse. As he approached, a passerby out for an evening stroll paused, studying him cautiously through the darkness. Yuri froze, gripped by fear, and instinctively hid the stick alongside his body. *Why am I afraid? I'm doing no wrong.* The stranger moved on, his footsteps quickly retreating. The delay was intolerable.

Driven by urgency, Yuri reached the blockhouse and pounded on the door. No response. Although weakened by weeks in prison, he was filled with rage. He planted his feet firmly on the ground, and with a swift movement, he threw his weight against the door. Wood creaked and cracked under the force but held. He looked around. Nobody. Again and again, he slammed into it. Pain shot through his arm; pain meant nothing. Sweat beaded on his forehead as he struck one final time. The door splintered at the lock and swung open.

Yuri stumbled inside, breathing heavily. "Zofia! Where are you?"

The sound of movement came from upstairs. Yuri closed the

blinds and flipped on the lights as he approached the stairs. "Zofia!" he called again, his voice a mix of desperation and fury.

"Yuri?" Zofia's voice called from the third floor. She and Sergei heard his footsteps mounting the stairs. "Yuri, be careful."

A locked door stood between them, a dim light spilling from the gap onto the landing.

"Sergei, let her go now," Yuri demanded, his voice choked with rage. No response.

Without hesitation, Yuri kicked the bedroom door open, sending splintered wood flying; however, he did not enter. Zofia stood in the room, her hair disheveled and the buttons of her blouse misaligned as she hurried to put on her shoes. Her face was a storm of emotions. Once dark, clear, and luminous, her eyes were now clouded by shadows of anger, guilt, and shame. And relief.

Once more, Zofia cautioned, "Yuri, be careful!"

Out of the gloom, Sergei stepped into the doorway, gripping a baseball bat. Yuri stepped back, raising his hands, feigning a clumsy retreat and bluffing fear. For a moment, Sergei's confidence swelled as he advanced, certain of his upper hand and that the ghost before him couldn't harm a hair on his head.

Then, Yuri struck. He rushed forward in a blur of movement, catching Sergei off guard. The blow swept Sergei backward, planting him on a table that then upended and broke apart with a crash. Before Sergei could recover, Yuri pinned him to the ground, straddling his chest. With feral intensity, he pressed his stick against Sergei's throat, his eyes aflame with unrestrained fury.

"Yuri, let's go! Don't hurt him! Don't kill him!" Zofia's voice cut through the chaos, rising with desperation. Sergei's struggles weakened as Yuri pushed harder against his throat, lost in the violent storm of his rage. "Yuri! Don't. Kill. Him." She cried again, her voice shrill with urgency.

Her words shattered the spell of his aggression like a lifeline pulling him back to humanity. The stick slipped from his grip, clattering to the floor. Yuri rose quickly, as though awakened. Sergei lay on his back, barely conscious, gasping for breath.

"Let's go. Hurry," Yuri urged.

On the tram, Zofia leaned close and whispered, "He's going to come after us. He will send the police."

Yuri responded coldly, "Let him. He will think twice when he realizes that we can accuse him of paying for your services."

His words stung Zofia. The bond of shared trust and respect had been lost. *Of course, he would know*, she thought. She couldn't hide.

Turning away, she pressed her lips together as tears burned her cheeks. She felt the shame of her spiritual nakedness. She wanted to say, "I'm sorry," but did not know to whom. She felt lost to forgiveness.

They rode in silence, exchanging no further words. Yuri sat rigidly, staring straight ahead until his hand brushed against the wad of paper in his pocket. The past came rushing back. He remembered.

NO RETURN

LATE SUMMER, 1972

The sun hid its face the following morning. Yuri examined his reflection in the mirror, improving it with scissors and a razor before finishing with soap and water. *There are more reasons than one for me to do this.* His shaking hands drew blood when he shaved. Through the mirror, he observed his sisters emerge from their bedroom. The warmth between them was gone. Zofia's face bore traces of recent tears and little sleep.

Petra appraised Yuri's transformed appearance and nodded in approval. Then, with questioning eyes, she glanced between Yuri and Zofia, probing for answers about the events of the night before. She remained silent.

After a simple meal, Yuri whispered to his sisters, "Be ready to meet outside."

They found a park bench under the shade of an oak and a lime tree. The towering *paneláky* east of their park bench cast a shadow that created a cooler microclimate, allowing the lime tree's blossoms to linger longer into the season. Their sweet, honey-like fragrance worked in vain to lift anyone's mood. Yuri placed a bucket on the ground and sat on it, facing his sisters. Zofia sat with her head in her hands.

Yuri said, "Before we talk, I need to know how much money we still have left."

Petra replied hastily, "About 750 crowns." She cast a questioning glance at Zofia, their recent source of household income. Zofia turned her head away, blushing and annoyed. "Rent is 550 crowns and is due next Friday evening. We're going to lose the apartment. What are we going to do?" Petra continued describing their destitution. She avoided Yuri's questioning eyes. Something wasn't adding up.

He then said, "Be ready to leave for Třeboň tonight. The train leaves at 11:00 PM. Your travel permits should be in order. I'll confirm when I meet the courier this afternoon. You'll travel under the cover of darkness. Pack light. Bring only what you can carry. Zofia, no books— they stay behind. Anything left will be lost. You'll arrive around 3:30 AM. I'll call the Krčméry family today; they'll meet you before first light." Yuri thought this news would bring them relief, but they appeared unmoved.

He added, "I have a little money. I don't know yet what I'll do with it. After paying the train fare, divide your remaining money between you."

Yuri scanned his surroundings with suspicion. A man sat on a park bench 50 meters away, a peculiar sight for this hour. He wore a parka. Yuri's breath came fast and shallow. Like a rising wind, the distant hum of an approaching tram sent a jolt through his body, his muscles tensing in anticipation of an unseen threat. Zofia gently took his hand, her voice a whisper against the noise. "Everything is okay. He can't hear us."

After opening his eyes and regaining control of his breathing, Yuri continued, "If you're wondering about *Táta*, I have no news. I never saw him. I don't know why they let me go. I expected worse. They treated me like I was a dangerous criminal. I expected to stay in jail for a long time, but they released me without warning or explanation." He paused, his voice softening. "It's good to be back. I didn't think I'd see this place again." A wave of sorrow accompanied the realization that his family was breaking apart at a time when he needed them most.

After wiping his eyes with his sleeve, Yuri asked about the news reports concerning their father. Petra answered, "All lies! They called him a traitor. They made him out to be a criminal who collaborated with Western nations. They invented stories of things that I can't even mention."

Looking up, Zofia finally spoke, softly and reluctantly. "Ivana's parents have a Tesla radio that picks up Radio Free Europe. I heard a broadcast condemning the government's suppression of the strike. They spoke of *Táta* and his friend as heroes. Remember the night before the strike, he mentioned that something good might come from speaking the truth. . . ." She trailed off, dispirited, bowing again, hiding her emptiness.

Petra, ignoring Zofia's inner turmoil, asked, "You haven't told me about last night."

Zofia remained silent. Yuri began recounting the events of the previous night in a quiet voice. "I was out of my mind," he admitted. "I could say my actions were justified, but it doesn't feel right. As usual, when I get angry, I go too far. I might have killed him if Zofia hadn't stopped me." He hesitated, reflecting. "I mean, I was no different from my tormentors in prison. It just crawled out of me. The same blind, uncontrollable rage. The same look in my eyes. I was ready to kill. The prison interrogators at least held back."

Petra frowned. "What are you talking about? That's absurd."

"No, I'm worse than they are. That's what I'm talking about," Yuri insisted more firmly, his brow furrowed.

"You're mad," Petra snapped, her patience wearing thin. She then recognized that he might still be struggling to distinguish reality from illusion. She glanced at Zofia for confirmation but received no response.

Yuri withstood her disagreement. "They taught us in school that evil lived 'out there'—always to the west. It had a face: the capitalist, the enemy. A different class of people. But *Maminka* never believed that. Remember. She said something different, quietly, never in front of others. She said 'The problem with evil lies within everyone's hearts.'"

Yuri turned to Zofia. "I shouldn't have gone to the strike. I should've stayed home. If I had, none of this would've happened. I regret it more than I can say." Zofia was unmoved, hiding.

Petra stood, growing annoyed with Yuri's speech. She looked at him with disbelief, as one might regard someone speaking in fevered delusion. "What are you talking about? What do you mean by all this religious-sounding talk? Are you suggesting there's something wrong with us, too? We didn't do anything wrong! If *Táta* hadn't agreed to become a strike leader, we'd still be living happy lives back in Třeboň. And what's with all this 'I regret it more than I can say' garbage? That's the same attitude that drove *Táta* to make such a stupid decision in the first place. If Zofia hadn't done what she did to get money, we would have starved."

Yuri turned to Petra and gazed at her with profoundly sad eyes. She tried to maintain composure, to hold his gaze, but couldn't. She felt herself withering inside. Something about him had changed. He was a different man.

He replied, the tone of his voice aching, "Did you never tell her to stop? Never tried to pull her back? You just took the money, kept your belly full while she sold herself. Like she was nothing more than a cow to be milked?"

Without a word, Petra stood up and walked away, her face flushed with anger. Zofia followed her with her eyes. Yuri stared straight ahead, unmoved.

Yuri asked Zofia gently, "Could you please tell me how all of this began between you and Sergei?"

Zofia looked up and stared across the ravine, the color in her cheeks revealing the sting of embarrassment. Several minutes passed. She straightened her back and began carefully, "You know we went to school together. Sergei was like a dream to me. I was *so* attracted to him, he was polished in his manners, handsome, and . . . very wealthy. Oh, how I wish I had never met him. He kept inviting me to his home to study, and I declined every time. I was cautious, as *Táta* had warned. He seemed so far above me, and I was scared of rejection, so I kept myself at a distance. He was always polite and gracious but persistent. Honestly, I enjoyed keeping the relationship in that kind of suspense.

"Then the strike happened. Petra and I were expelled from school. I missed seeing him and the attention he gave me, and Petra and I began to run out of money. One day, he called, and I told him everything about our struggles, about how desperate we were. That was a mistake. We agreed to meet in the ravine. He was kind but so blunt. He proposed a 'transactional' relationship, if you know what I mean. I couldn't believe it. I became furious and walked away. He said nothing. He knew of my contraband books—that's right, I accidentally told him—and I was afraid he would leverage this knowledge against me.

"Our need for money became more acute. We were low on food. I became afraid he would report us to the secret police about the books. I don't know why I thought this; you know how it is, you feel you can never trust anyone. We had no idea if or when you or *Táta* would return. We were running out of money. Sergei sent me a letter inviting me to reconsider his offer. And I did. I gave in and went to him." Tears welled in her eyes. She continued while weeping, the pitch of her voice rising, "I'm like you. I feel dirty. I didn't listen to *Táta's* advice when he told us, 'On the outside, people look one way. But on the inside? It's not the same.' I keep remembering his words.

"Did Petra tell you that we were barely getting by? That's not true. We eventually had plenty of money coming in, and we now have over 6,000 crowns. She tried to cover that up.

"To make matters worse for me, I eventually had moments of genuine intimacy with him," Zofia confessed. Yuri looked down, embarrassed. She continued, "At first, I hated what I was doing. I acted cold and detached. But over time, I began to have feelings for him. . . . And he also paid me well, so I wanted to keep it coming. I can't believe I did this . . . I wish I could yank up the past by its roots and throw it away." She paused, her voice distraught. "When you showed up last night . . . at first, I felt disappointed, angry, even. But when he wouldn't let me go, when he picked up that bat to fight you, I awakened from this nightmare. . . . I feel so empty." Zofia looked up into the sky, blinking away her tears.

They sat in silence for a while, the stillness between them heavy. Yuri shifted on the park bench. "That's enough, Zofia. I have nothing to say. Thank you for your answer. I need to meet this courier. When you return home, please remind Petra to start packing. What happened with Sergei last night may blow up in my face."

Zofia asked softly, "You mentioned the name Alyosha earlier. Could you please tell me about him?"

Yuri glanced at his watch and then looked away into the distance, agitated. The question drew him toward dangerous memories he wished to remain buried. "Right . . . Alyosha," he said, his voice agitated. "He was a religious dissident—a leader in an underground church network.

A kind, brave man. I don't see any hope for him. They tortured me a little. They tortured him far more."

"Oh, Yuri, did they torture you?" Zofia asked.

Yuri's voice wavered as he replied, "Yes, Zofia. We can talk more about it some other time. Alyosha, though . . . he suffered far more. They interrogated and tortured him repeatedly, trying to force him to reveal other leaders in the underground church. He never did. He never will. He actually knew Father Kaleda."

Yuri paused, gathering his thoughts. "Even before they arrested him, he seemed to know what was coming. He prepared himself. He memorized long portions of the New Testament and Psalms. Even in prison, I would hear him, lisping quietly, pacing back and forth, whispering the words he'd stored in his heart. He told me this was a real treasure. He ordered his days with prayer. Hours of it. For his captors, too. What else could he do? And he sang. He said it kept the despair away . . . while I was sinking into it."

Yuri's voice softened. "He cared for me. He gave up the one bed we had. He slept on the hard floor so I could recover from sessions of torture. And he'd been through the same. When I was starving, he gave me his portion. We were both wasting away, but he didn't hesitate. I was a stranger to him, but he treated me as a . . ." Yuri stopped, unable to finish.

"It was like he lived on a different plane," Yuri said. "He suffered terribly—his body broken, his family left to endure sorrow I can't imagine. And still, he found joy.

"Sometimes, he fell into despair. He'd sit on the floor for hours, not moving. But he always came back. He'd start singing. Thanking God for the prison. He said it was preparing him for 'an eternal weight of glory.' Things like that.

"I sometimes think of him as 'Crazy Alyosha.' Yet, of everyone I've ever known, I've never met anyone more . . . I don't know, so childlike, so un-crazy. He was a man at peace, even while living in hell.

"Still, I saw other innocent men condemned, too. I saw lives torn apart for nothing. And so, despite Alyosha's example, I question the existence of a moral God. It's the same old reason, too much pain in the world. I've got to go now. Will you take my bucket home for me?"

Yuri began walking across the ravine, lamenting Zofia's woeful story, Petra's strange outburst of anger, and thinking especially about her deception concerning the money. He couldn't remember when she had lied to him in the past. How much more pain could be added to him? *No wonder they weren't relieved when I told them about the train tickets. I wouldn't have taken any money even if she offered.* He couldn't endure further fragmentation of the family.

The man in the parka rushed toward him. Yuri stopped and took a defensive stance, prepared for confrontation.

"I'm sorry to bother you," the man fumbled, his voice low. "I'm Ivana's father, Alexei Beneš. I want to say how much I appreciate what you and your father have done. It gives us hope. I don't believe a word of the official news reports, but you need to be careful. I've noticed unusual cars parked around our apartment building, and other things, like strange 'maintenance workers' who don't seem to belong."

He hesitated, glancing around nervously. "My apartment number is 425. If you ever need help, come find me. And . . . I'm sorry about my parka. You understand I had to wear it." Without waiting for a reply, Alexei turned and hurried away. Yuri watched him depart, smiling at this curiosity.

Days after Zofia and Petra's departure, Ivana knocked on the door. With her characteristic lilting voice, she said, "Hi, Mr. Yuri. I miss Zofia."

Yuri knelt and offered her a gentle hug. "I know, Ivana, so do I. But I have something for you." He pointed to a stack of contraband books on the floor. "She left these behind. Ask your parents if they would like to keep them for her. And shhh, can you keep a secret from your friends? We shouldn't discuss it any further."

Ivana nodded solemnly, with large eyes that spoke, "You can trust me," and walked away, flapping her arms like a bird. Yuri leaned against the doorframe, watching her until she disappeared, then slid down to the floor. He was wasting away the nights and weeping away the days, like some homesick soul from an old story he barely remembered. His life was unraveling—he had fears within, and there were dangers without. He felt the keen sting of isolation from the lively company of his family. He was alone in the world. He had no work permit, money was running out, he wouldn't accept any from Zofia, and the need to abandon the apartment grew closer with every passing day. He worried about retaliation from Sergei, or worse, another arrest. The way forward was unclear, and guilt consumed his conscience. He recalled the solitary kestrel he had seen from the train to Brno months ago and began to grasp the meaning of this dark omen.

'Oh, that I had wings like a dove! I would fly away and be at rest.' Alyosha often prayed these words from a psalm, and Yuri found himself repeating them now by rote, if only for the small comfort of distraction. He swayed on the floor, recalling the starlings he had seen on the train to Brno. "Oh, that I had wings like a dove! I would fly

away and be at rest. " He repeated these words like a ruminating cow, seeking solace in their sound and rhythm rather than their meaning.

But the meaning slipped through. He admired their defiance and whispered in a quiet challenge to God, "Lord, if you exist, please let me be like the bird that finds rest." A moment later, his stomach reminded him he was hungry, and he rose and plodded off to fetch the mail.

Returning to the apartment, Yuri opened a letter from Zofia. All was well. She wrote about working long hours during the July harvest, haymaking, and how the fresh air and exercise had brought them joy and refreshment. *I'm glad they were able to fly away. No word from Petra. She probably still hates me.* In closing, Zofia had added: "Oh, Thor is here! He just appeared a couple of days ago. We're taking care of him."

This news stunned Yuri. *Something has happened to Father Kaleda!*

A knock at the door interrupted his thoughts. Yuri was in no frame of mind to take precautions. This time, it was Ivana and her father. Alexei Beneš whispered, "Can we talk in the ravine?"

In the quiet of the ravine, Alexei introduced himself again, without the parka. "Ivana misses Zofia terribly. We're considering applying for a travel permit for my wife, Ivana, and me to visit them in Třeboň. I know it's risky, and I'm guessing you can't travel legally, but I wanted to invite you to come with us. There might be safety in numbers."

Yuri weighed the offer. His forged travel permit was soon to expire. *Whatever choice I make, there's no turning back*, he realized. Staying meant hardship, humiliation, and isolation—Zetor refused to hire him. No business in the city would hire him; he was denied a work permit. Leaving meant living as a fugitive. He looked at Alexei and said, "What else can I do? Yes, I'll be ready to fly."

FLIGHT

EARLY FALL, 1972

He traveled by night train, disappearing from Brno like steam over a pot. The train car felt like a cocoon, a momentary sanctuary from trouble—except for one thing. Yuri was periodically awakened by a plainclothes security officer who demanded his permit. The memory of his imprisonment remained painfully vivid, making the charade of remaining calm nearly unbearable. In those moments, he silently repeated the phrases Alyosha had taught him, commanding his body not to sweat drops of blood.

The train arrived in Třeboň at 3:35 a.m. The city was asleep. Ivana rested in her father's arms as Yuri parted from them. Her parents wished him safe travels. They would meet again. He passed through the shadows of night on foot, invisible to all, immensely relieved to be rid of suspicious eyes. His life as a fugitive was driven by raw urgency; at this hour, he was nearly spent.

As he approached the farm, he set his duffel bag down to rest and to breathe in the new day. A chorus of birds awakened the dawn. A gentle breeze pushed against an unlatched garden gate, producing a creaking noise and carrying the familiar fragrance of soil and animals. In the distance, he heard the hum of a lone tractor driven by an urgent farmer. With no time for rest, every moment counted. For an instant, he felt an intermission from constant fear, a return to Beauty—much like the day he delivered Thor to Father Kaleda. It seemed so long ago. Then, he mistrusted these fleeting sensations; now, he embraced them as a healing balm.

As Yuri walked along streams bordered by thick raspberry bushes, he picked the ripe fruit in the light of the setting moon. Ferns were turning brown. Apple trees, with branches bowed under the weight of their fruit, lined the roadside. He gathered apples from low-hanging branches and the ground below, adding weight to his duffel bag. Gazing down the tree-lined road, he thought of the people who planted these trees years ago. *What kind of world was this, where people would plant trees merely to sustain destitute wanderers?* Nearing the collective farm, he ached for the life forever out of reach. But right now, he needed a place to hide and to think.

He proceeded quietly to the mechanics' workshop, careful not to arouse the farm dogs. He passed a couple of Zetor tractors awaiting repair. With the key still in his possession, he unlocked the door and slipped inside. The familiar scent of diesel fuel and oil flooded him with memories of years spent working alongside his father. Sorrow returned. He missed his father. He set his bag on a bench, ate his fruit, and then lay his head on the bag. He meant to plan his next steps, but sleep overtook him.

The partially ajar door creaked as it opened and closed, waking Yuri. The faint light of dawn briefly entered the workshop, intensifying his fears before they subsided. A dog licked Yuri's face, whimpering with pure joy, its tail wagging madly.

"Thor, my favorite dog."

Yuri filled up his deficit of affection for Thor, giving him an accounting of why he had been away so long. Pardon was freely granted.

Time passed with Thor faithfully at his master's side while Yuri remained paralyzed by indecision. He spoke to Thor about his troubles. He asked him about Father Kaleda. He knew he had to reach Kolence, the home of Father Kaleda. Suddenly, a call rang out:

"Thor, come!"

It was the voice of Petra.

Thor looked up at Yuri, snorted once, nudged open the door with his muzzle, and vanished. Yuri peeked through the cracked door, watching Petra far off, squatting to greet Thor. He saw her stand, look toward the workshop, then disappear into the *kolchoz*.

The menacing song of nightingales filled the air as the sun peeked over the horizon. The dawn had become a threat; he bade farewell to the darkness. Yuri knew the workshop would soon fill with mechanics. He didn't know who had replaced his father or where their sympathies lay. Digging through his bag for another apple, he paused and stared at Kaleda's envelope.

He quickly closed his bag. The door opened quietly, startling Yuri as Zofia and Thor walked in. The dog rushed forward, eager to be near Yuri again, proud of his role in reuniting brother and sister.

"Yuri! It's so good to see you! How did you get here?" Zofia exclaimed as they embraced.

In the dawn's light, Yuri noticed a decline in Zofia's vitality: her once-lustrous hair was now unruly and disheveled, and her piercing eyes were clouded and heavy. But that wasn't it. Sorrow and regret had drawn a veil over her beauty. She sensed his scrutiny and turned away, ashamed, reading his thoughts.

"I arrived on the night train. Ivana and her parents also came along. Ivana misses you . . . and so do I. They should be here soon, I think, after finding lodging. I had a forged travel pass about to expire, so I had no choice but to come. I'm hungry. Do you have any food?"

They left the workshop together, Yuri moving with the slouch of a hunted creature, hugging the shadows, wary of what might be lurking behind the darkened windows above and around him. "Act like you own the place, not like a hunted creature," Zofia urged. He had to trust Zofia that this passage and asylum with the Krčméry family was indeed safe. They paused at the entrance of an apartment unit, casually standing, engaging in non-essential conversation while looking about for any unknown threats.

Upon vanishing into the *kolchozní domy*, Yuri was surprised when the Krčméry family greeted him with unexpected warmth. They had followed the news of the strike and believed that the leaders, including Yuri, were *not* confirmed enemies of the State. They had become accustomed to reaching conclusions opposite to those promoted by the State media. Petra's welcome and embrace were cordial but restrained.

Thor never left Yuri's side.

The simple farmer's meal tasted ambrosial to Yuri; it was the first satisfying meal he had enjoyed in months. He shared the remaining apples he had been hoarding, and they were gratefully received.

As the day wore on, the Krčméry family showed no concern about sheltering a fugitive, but Yuri knew he couldn't impose on their kindness much longer. He brooded alone in a corner, staring out the window, strategizing but finding no answers.

Everyone was away, at work or school, except for Zofia, who stayed behind to welcome Ivana's family. Although travel permits for domestic travel were not strictly enforced, the 14-kilometer journey to Kolence still posed a significant hurdle. Most people didn't own personal vehicles.

"Why do I need to go to Kolence, anyway?" he asked himself, unable to shake the sense that the journey was urgent despite his doubts. "Maybe Thor just wanted to come look for me."

When the Beneš family arrived, Zofia welcomed them and kept them engaged with food and conversation. Meanwhile, Ivana wandered around, exploring and examining books, but found little of interest.

"Hi, Mr. Yuri. What's the name of your dog?"

Yuri held his envelope, gazing out the window, his thoughts wandering unproductively. Thor's tail thumped against the floor in warm approval of the sweet vision. Yuri turned to her and said, "Hi, Ivana. I hope you had a nice trip. I'm sorry to be rude. I'm just thinking. This is my dog, Thor."

Sensing his evasiveness and sadness, she resolved to press further.

"Hi, Thor. You're a good dog," she said, prompting more tail thumping. Thor swiveled his head on the wooden floor to face her, raising his eyebrows as if to acknowledge her attention.

"What is Mr. Yuri thinking about, Mr. Thor?"

Yuri turned to Thor, amused by her kind-hearted persistence.

"Thor, tell Ivana I need to reach a small town called Kolence. Something has happened to an old friend of mine. I think."

"Why don't you just take the bus?" she asked.

"Bus? There is no bus service in this city."

"Oh. I didn't know that. But I saw a bus this morning. It was at the train station."

Thor turned to look at Yuri as if urging him to consider her words.

Intrigued, Yuri confirmed it by questioning the others and soon found himself studying a bus schedule Ivana's mother had obtained. Travel restrictions to Kolence had been relaxed.

RANSACKED

EARLY FALL, 1972

After lunch, Yuri traveled to Kolence with Zofia and Ivana. The bus's old body squeaked and rattled as they lumbered down the bumpy road. Ivana delighted in the springy seats, laughing often; her weight perfectly matched the strength of the springs for maximum bounce whenever they hit a pothole. "I'm flying!" she squealed.

The bus slowed to a stop, and its brakes let out one final, drawn-out hiss. All three tumbled out into the daylight.

They heard the bus's brakes release and the crunch of its wheels on the gravel. They watched it depart, trailing a plume of dark exhaust. Above, billowing cumulus clouds cast a shifting interplay of light and shadow over the rural landscape.

"We need to move fast to catch the return bus," said Yuri.

As they strolled through the village, memories of a happy childhood deepened Zofia's sorrow. A break in the clouds lit up the familiar fence lines and gardens—her favorite hiding spots from when she played *schovávaná*. She once played shop with Petra and their friends, using stones, leaves, and homemade paper money. She was painfully reminded of her childhood innocence.

"You never told me *why* you had to come to Třeboň," Zofia asked.

"Remember when you wrote, 'Thor is here'? I had to come. Something has happened to Father Kaleda. When I brought Thor to him a over a year ago, he told me he might be arrested soon."

"I didn't know you were that close to him. You've been fidgeting with that envelope in your pocket. What's inside it?"

"He gave it to me before I left. I don't know what's inside. Somehow, he knew I'd come back here; he told me to bring it when I did. Strange. And now here we are, just like he said. There were times when I nearly burned it."

The closer he approached Father Kaleda's cottage, the more Yuri questioned his decision to come. He dreaded what he might discover, made more acute by his recent imprisonment.

After gaining their bearings, Yuri led Zofia and Ivana past the old church building to the cemetery. "I want to show you something." Zofia was reluctant to follow. They found their mother's gravestone.

This was unexpected for Zofia. She ran her fingers through her hair, breathing deeply, recalling her mother's touch—morning brushes, nightly hugs, and prayers. The memory of her and Petra huddled together while their mother read aloud reminded her of where her love for books had begun. Now, standing at the burial site for the first time since her death, the finality of loss struck her with a fresh, raw intensity. Torn away. Forever.

She remembered one day she and Petra decorated their mother's sick room with flowers, hoping to cure her illness with kindness. . . .

Spring weather held a slim promise of relief for Jana Dvořák. The warmer temperatures, it was hoped, would palliate her chills. Her coughing and labored breathing haunted everyone with their reminders of her struggle between life and death. Bedridden, she awakened to the wind whispering against the window, groaning louder as the blowing increased. The wind brought the faint smell of fermenting silage into her room. She listened for the sound of their voices or their movements. Nothing. *Where have they gone?*

Petra, 14, and Zofia, 15, paused their routine morning chores and ran barefoot to the edge of the forest bordering the farm to gather wood anemones. They dared each other to go barefoot. When both accepted, they raced to their destination. Petra always won. As they crossed the fields on their return, they collected yellow cowslips, just beginning to bloom.

"Ack!" Petra exclaimed, carefully dodging where cows had left their marks, dark and flat upon the earth.

"Ack!" Zofia replied in sympathetic understanding.

Returning home, they stripped the lower leaves and arranged the flowers in small cups of water, quietly placing them on the windowsills and tabletops of their mother's room. They asked, "Can you see them if we put them here?"

"Yes. I love your flowers. I didn't know they were blooming. I should have known. Thank you. Look, you even went outside barefoot. Do you smell the cowslip? I wish . . ." She was short of breath. Her voice weakened, and she broke into another fit of coughing.

"You girls remember to cover your mouths when you enter my room. . . . Where is your father?" She asked, recovering her breath.

Petra answered, "He's out. He left before we were awake. Again."

Jana whispered to herself, "He'll never forgive himself."

. . . Zofia looked at the flowers laid on the graves, many of them made of plastic. The artificial flowers on neighboring graves and the absence of fresh flowers on her mother's grave troubled her.

Zofia broke the silence. "What are you going to do? I mean, how will you survive? You can't go back to the *byt* in Brno. You're a fugitive now, aren't you?"

"I don't know. Maybe I'll stay with Father Kaleda. Somehow, he survives."

Moss and lichen had taken hold of the north-facing side of the concrete gravestone. Cracks had appeared, and some parts had flaked off. Yuri bent down to pull up the weeds that insisted on covering the base of the stone.

"I want to show you something," he said, directing Zofia's attention to the inscription.

> We all like sheep have gone astray
> each of us has turned to his own way
> and the Lord has laid on Him
> the iniquity of us all.
> —Isaiah 53:6

They both silently reflected on the words. Zofia initially avoided the meaning, fearing they would evoke more painful memories. She looked away into the distance.

Eventually, she quietly shared her observations with Yuri about the other gravestones, noting that most were made of granite and well-tended by the residents of Kolence, with flowers and candles—some still burning. She remarked that the granite gravestones bore few inscriptions, usually just family names and dates, as though the mourners had spent much on the marker but economized on the engraving. She added that *Maminka* did the opposite: she chose an inexpensive concrete gravestone, as if conveying a message to the living mattered more than leaving behind a beautiful, indestructible, mute stone.

"We probably heard these words as children," Yuri mused, "but we didn't listen. Do you understand them? They must have been important to *Maminka*. Why do you think she chose these words?"

Zofia had not yet caught up emotionally to Yuri at the sight of their *Maminka's* grave. This place served as a focal point for long-suppressed memories. With each breath, she inhaled another memory of her Maminka's illness, the crushed hope for her recovery, her burial, and the days of emptiness that followed. She was ashamed at what she had become, as though her mother was still a living presence. Finally, she once again forced her gaze back upon the tombstone.

After a long silence, Zofia finally responded, "She probably hoped we would visit her grave one day—likely much sooner than after five years. Or maybe she hoped some lonely wanderer would stop to read it. That's something she would want; she cared for strangers, no? She knew her life was ending, and this is what she wanted the world to remember. . . ."

Yuri said, "For strangers or maybe her own children."

Zofia became agitated and shifted about as though she wanted to leave.

"What does 'gone astray' mean?" Ivana asked, interrupting. They had forgotten about her.

"It means to wander off and get lost. Don't get lost," Zofia commanded, offering her a gentle smile and leveraging the force of her expressive eyes.

Ivana returned a mischievous half-smile and gave an indifferent shrug before wandering off.

"I feel like a lost sheep. I have no home," Yuri said.

As much as Zofia wanted to walk away and forget, her mother's felt presence forbade her. And she couldn't resist pointing out Yuri's literary dullness. "But think about the whole verse: 'Going astray' doesn't mean getting lost in the ordinary sense—it's about 'the iniquity of us all.'"

They stood in silence for a moment, the weight of their shared guilt pressing down on them. Until now, 'iniquity' had been a meaningless word. It was a taboo subject. This was the kind of language they had been repelled by.

A bee landed on a plastic flower in a vase at a neighboring grave, finding no nourishment.

Zofia spoke again, "You understand, don't you, why *Táta* risked so much for the strike? Maminka's death haunted him. That memory became a curse. In the end, he tried to erase his accusing conscience by destroying his domestic life. He was driven by guilt. What is guilt when there is no God? Yet I feel the same way."

Stooping down, she pointed to the bee. "Look at this little bee, unable to find nourishment from a plastic flower. I am this bee. My heart needs nourishment, and the world is a plastic flower. Yuri, I can understand *Táta's* self-sacrifice at Zetor. Sometimes I feel I'd do anything to quiet my conscience, too."

"Baa-baa," came Ivana's playful voice as she wandered among the tombstones, lightening Zofia's dark mood.

Yuri and Zofia looked up, puzzled.

Yuri said, "Remember when we were last in Brno? I reminded you and Petra of what *Maminka* taught: the problem with evil lies within our hearts."

"I remember. And Petra didn't care for your comment—especially the part about her milking a cow," Zofia said. "Look at the other gravestones. Only a few bear a cross on top. It must have been an act of political resistance for *Maminka* to request a bold cross on hers. Almost all the older gravestones bear crosses, but the newer ones do not—probably since the failure of the Prague Spring. Why did a cross become such a problem?"

Yuri replied, "Do you remember how they taught us in school that Christians were fools for accepting suffering and injustice? They said Christians are like lambs. The cross was a symbol of their weakness. The New Faith taught us to fight back against exploitation. But lambs don't fight against Nazis and Capitalists. And lambs don't build a socialist society. So they mocked the lambs. Silenced them. No one wanted to be a lamb. So no crosses."

"Baa," Ivana called out from farther away.

Zofia smiled, "That silly one. She's pretending to be a lost sheep. . . . Maybe. Remember *Maminka* would say things like 'Jesus died for our sins.' We were never taught 'He died to set an example.'

Yuri replied. "That's what the cross means, Zofia. It's *not* just Jesus setting an example. Look at what it says: 'The Lord has laid on *him* the iniquity of us all.' It's about the Lord being punished in the place of others. That's not 'weakness'. Either we bear the guilt, or he does in our place. I remember Father Kaleda saying things like this."

They both paused to consider this.

"But if this verse is true, then it's more than just a nice bit of poetry," Zofia responded. "But how can an *event* that happened so long ago have *meaning* for us now?"

After some thought, Yuri said, "We should get going if we're going to catch the last bus home. Ivana, come back here."

Ivana returned, looking sheepish.

Zofia and Yuri suppressed their amusement, but who can hide a smile from a little girl? She burst into laughter, delighted by her own shenanigans.

"Zofia, you look pretty today," Ivana said, smiling.

Zofia's hands instinctively rose to her hair, her fingers moving with a practiced motion. As she walked, she pondered Ivana's innocent remark and her conversation with Yuri.

They walked quietly through the village of Kolence, trying to remember where their family had once lived. The passage of time was evident everywhere: Many homes had been abandoned or left to decay, casualties of farm collectivization and urban migration. Most houses were weathered to a uniform grey, their pastel paint long faded or peeling, and the plaster fell away, exposing the underlying brick. Vines now covered neglected wood piles.

Yuri recalled a story. "Do you remember *Táta* saying that *Maminka* was a teetotaler? No beer, nothing. He told me this story: Every fall, the community would harvest apples along the roadside.

Someone had a press, and we'd collect a few gallons of cider. Most of it went into the cellar, but *Maminka* would leave a couple of gallons on the porch until 'it was just right.' She didn't know why it made her feel so good."

Zofia chuckled.

Yuri continued to lead the way to Father Kaleda's cottage. Each of them was lost in thought. Yuri's mind kept drifting back to the verse from the graveyard. It was good news, yet hard to believe. Still, he tried to understand, he longed to believe, even if it were only a comforting fiction to ease the pain of reality.

He glanced sideways at Zofia, and Ivana's words rang true—her beauty had indeed returned, radiant despite the neglect of her wild, unruly hair. Her renewed spirit was most apparent in her eyes.

"Are you doing alright?" Yuri asked.

"Yes, I'm fine now," Zofia replied.

They walked the familiar path that led to Kaleda's cottage. Under the shadows of large evergreens and chestnut trees, Yuri observed the handiwork of cruelty: a door swinging on its hinges and the remnants of Kaleda's humble lifestyle scattered around the outside of the cottage. The very thing Yuri feared most had come to pass.

What evil would crush the life of such a harmless, virtuous man? What threat was he to anyone? Yuri wondered.

Following Yuri's lead, all three sat on the entrance step. For a fleeting moment, Yuri gazed at the envelope he had held for so long, tapping it against his hand before opening it and beginning to read it.

> If you are reading this letter, it's likely that I, <u>Jan Kaleda</u>, have been arrested for crimes against the state. My activities in disseminating Christian literature have been interpreted as resistance to the government, and I will probably be charged with 'Incitement Against the State.' To whoever reads this letter, you have been chosen to be entrusted with continuing the work of creating samizdat for the underground Christian community in the Southern Bohemian Region. If you choose to accept this responsibility, you are participating in a tradition of succession and inviting upon yourself this danger.

Enclosed is a map with directions to the
small, underground bytové dílny. There,
you'll find typewriters, mimeographs,
cassette duplicators, and all the materials
needed for producing literature. Other
parties are involved in this operation,
although you will never know who they are.
They will be watching the cottage for a new
inhabitant and will provide you with your
daily bread. The map includes the location
of a small box away from the cottage,
where you will receive instructions on
what is needed or how to request supplies.
They will supply you with materials for
publishing documents at another location,
and you will drop off the completed
documents at yet another site. Refer to the
enclosed maps. If it snows or the ground is
muddy from rain, do not try to backtrail
them.

     If you accept this responsibility,
you also will be in danger of arrest. If
not, destroy this letter. There are other
means by which this work will be carried
out. Your first responsibility will be to
reproduce this letter to give to another
whom you trust as worthy when your life is
in danger.

The grass withers, the flower fades,

But the word of our God stands forever.
—Is 40:8

Yuri was stunned. He whispered, "'When your life is in danger.' How can this be? How could Father Kaleda have trusted me with something like this? Who would accept such a task? Do you remember how he'd say things, and you'd think, how does he know that will happen, and then it happens?"

Zofia asked, "No. What will you do? You're going to dig yourself into a deeper hole than the one you're already in. Producing samizdat is a subversive activity. Look what they did to Father Kaleda."

After a long pause, Yuri replied, "What else can I do? My life is already in danger. Didn't you do the same, sort of, with the books you transcribed?"

"No, it was different. But what interest do you have in producing Christian literature?"

"What else can I do?" he said, agitated. "Besides, my interest has grown."

"Aren't you worried you might be arrested again?"

"Yes," Yuri answered. "I'm finished with Marxism. Sure, I'm worried about it. But more than that, I want to cut it down. You could say, 'like father, like son.' But there's something more that outweighs my fears. If Father Kaleda was willing to risk his life for something he believed in, then maybe it's true. If Alyosha's life was changed so deeply by his faith, I want to believe it too. Their courage and suffering—it spoke to me. It was like a seal, like the stamp on a travel permit, marking what they believed to be authentic. So maybe it's worth the risk. I'll do it for Kaleda and Alyosha. And *Maminka*. If just one verse from the Bible on my *Maminka's* grave could bring me a little hope, then I want to read more and do more. What other option do I have?

"I can come and visit," Zofia responded timidly. "But how will you survive?"

"Do you see those two chestnut trees and all the chestnuts scattered beneath them? I could survive a whole year on just those."

Zofia looked at him to determine whether he was serious.

"But the letter said I would receive my daily bread. I don't know where else to turn. Still, just in case, please come tomorrow with food and my duffel bag. I remember something Alyosha said when I worried for you and Petra while in prison. He reminded me, 'Look at the birds of the air; they do not sow or reap or store away in barns, and yet our Heavenly Father feeds them.' At the time, I thought he was half-mad. Then later, I memorized what he said. And now. . . ."

Yuri, Zofia, and Ivana worked together to gather Father Kaleda's modest belongings and restore order to the cottage. Yuri embraced Zofia and Ivana before they departed for home.

As night fell, the flicker of a lamp in the window signaled his presence. Later in the evening, as he stepped outside to fetch water from the pump, he discovered a basket of food left on the doorstep—a surprising reassurance that he was not alone in this new chapter of his life.

SUCCESSION

FALL INTO LATE WINTER, 1973

The familiar cottage stood apart from the village of Kolence, guarded by trees. Moss covered the northern slope of the roof so thickly that small trees and mushrooms had begun to take root. Originally built as a vacation retreat and later adopted as a parsonage for Father Kaleda, it was never intended to be a permanent residence. Yuri wandered through the quiet, lonely space, the wood floor squeaking, keeping company with two mice, gradually coming to terms with what would become his new home. He cleaned out the wood-burning stove and taught himself how to build a fire. Early failed attempts filled the cottage with smoke. After sunset, the unusual darkness and quiet unsettled him and filled him with longing for his family. The chirring of crickets, near and far, was his only companion. Throughout the first night, he woke often, startled by the sound of dead branches falling onto the wooden shingles as a rare autumn wind swept through the trees.

At dawn, he unlatched the windows, feeling the crisp morning air rush in, smelling coal smoke from distant neighbors, and inadvertently allowing a stray housefly or moth inside—the last survivors of the season. His gaze lingered on the woodpile in a lean-to outside, now nearly depleted. He'd have to chop more soon, but the noise would attract attention—attention he couldn't afford.

A loyal co-laborer left Yuri's daily provisions by the door each evening. In addition, he included a note requesting specific items of samizdat. He tried to catch a glimpse of this elusive friend, if only to thank him. If only to make human contact. The courier's silent hand and secretive movements reminded Yuri that he could not fully surrender to the serenity of the picturesque surroundings—soon to be ablaze with golden yellows, deep oranges, and fiery reds. This secluded cottage, hidden deep within the trees, so peaceful, had once been discovered and staked out. *Plundered. Arrested.*

Not long ago, the *státní bezpečnost* had stormed in, ransacked the place, and violently arrested his friend. Someone had talked. Someone close. Yuri shuddered at the memory of his friend's arrest and the sickening certainty that it could happen again, this time with greater cruelty.

One day, Yuri's solitude was interrupted. He immediately recognized Zofia's gentle, cautious touch on the iron door knocker. He opened the door to find Zofia and Petra standing there, with Thor eagerly beside them. "Thor! It's so good to see you, old boy!" Yuri exclaimed as he collapsed onto the floor, quickly engaging in a playful wrestle with his old dog.

Zofia crossed her arms.

"You're not glad to see us?"

Yuri looked up. He laughed, embarrassed.

"Sure," he said. "I'm glad to see you."

Thor took strategic advantage of this distraction and pinned Yuri to the ground, tail wagging in triumph.

"I need Thor as a watchdog," Yuri said after he stood and embraced his sisters. Zofia saw a trace of concern cross his face.

"You look tired. Is something wrong?" she asked.

"I'm happy to see you," Yuri said, his tone turning more serious. "But I worry that the *státní bezpečnost* may have followed you. Maybe when you come again, you should take different routes."

Petra's vacant expression revealed her struggle to understand Yuri's peculiar way of living. The memory of their father's rebellion still lingered, its consequences painfully fresh. And now this. She didn't want any part of it. To her, a life devoid of physical labor and contribution to the collective felt pointless—a wasted life. *Why not come out of hiding and find a place to stay on the farm?* She thought. She remembered the small vegetable garden she had once tended on the apartment balcony and how Yuri, after long shifts at the factory, had carried lumber and soil up four flights of stairs to help her bring a bit of the farm into the city. That's the brother she wanted back.

The girls brought good news from the collective farm in Třeboň. The Krčméry family had worked discreetly, listening to some and subtly planting ideas in others about the sisters; at times, battles had to be fought and bribes paid. Gradually, the tide of opinion shifted in their favor. Whispers grew into conversations, and soon, the collective will of the farmers had the power to bend and eventually overrule the rigid bureaucracy. The sisters successfully secured residency and, consequently, their security. Yuri dropped his head in thankful relief at such good news. His sisters fell silent, turning their thoughts to their brother, who, in contrast, would remain unseen, unknown, and eventually—hopefully—forgotten.

Later that afternoon, upon returning to Třeboň, Petra's fears were heightened when the bus driver asked, "*Slečna*, have you forgotten to bring your dog?" The seemingly simple question unsettled them both, and for Petra, the fear and harsh reality of Yuri's situation were too much to endure. She never returned to see him again.

Yuri resolved to begin the work, note in hand from the mysterious courier, despite having little understanding of what it would entail. The map enclosed in the envelope from Father Kaleda led him to a subterranean room cleverly hidden beneath the floor. He carried two kerosene lamps. The walls were of thick stone, and the air was cool, carrying a faintly sweet smell of earth and mold. The space was outfitted with everything he needed to produce banned literature for the underground church. He stood viewing in the dim lamplight rough wooden shelves, hastily assembled, lining the walls, holding a carefully curated collection of books and religious texts: copies of the Bible, theological commentaries, and writings by Christian thinkers and dissenters. It was a world apart from repairing or building tractors.

The steady demand for document production provided a welcome distraction, drawing his mind away from the fear of arrest. He imagined the mingled feelings of joy and danger as the banned documents moved through the underground network and finally reached their destination, where they were received with gratitude.

Above, Thor kept a faithful watch, occasionally breaking the silence with a bark—typically a false alarm triggered by a red squirrel. Yuri conceded the advantages of practicing quick evacuations. Breathlessly, after evacuating his subterranean workshop and erasing all evidence from above of what was hidden below, he would say to himself, "Ah, of course, another squirrel. Dangerous creatures. Can't be too careful."

Initially, the work overwhelmed him as he fumbled about. The typewriter keys clacked and thudded slowly as he hunted and pecked. Zofia proved indispensable during those early days with her nimble fingers, helping him meet the increasing demand on her occasional visits. She swiftly produced multiple mimeograph templates for each new order. The mimeograph seemed a miracle to her, having copied many books by hand. Despite the risks of her presence, Yuri cherished these days of working together.

The two were like moths drawn to a flame, irresistibly captivated by its light and danger. Defying the fury and power of the state by producing banned literature held a strange allure, and serving the underground church gave their work significance. The irony did not escape Yuri that he and Zofia had a distant relationship with the church. He often asked himself why he did this work. It was partly for survival, but also for something more. His mind often escaped to the past and the little community that Father Kaleda shepherded. The chords of nostalgia from the past harmonized with the sweetness of the present labor. The emptiness and longing he felt for Kaleda's community were a kind of pain he cherished—proof he was alive inside. Or had become alive.

Zofia reluctantly left her work behind at sunset, undeterred by the risks. But she was not unseen. Passing through Kolence on foot, a few villagers peered from behind darkened windows, their watchful eyes following her every step. Whispers circulated behind closed doors—rumors about the young woman at the bus stop, vanishing into the countryside. Carrying secrets.

"Mm, mm. Trouble."

"Down by the forest road—strange things, they've been goin' on."

Though Yuri kept himself busy, the silence of the long evenings pressed in on him. The cheerful conversations he once shared with his sisters in Brno had faded into distant memory, and Zofia's visits had become more infrequent out of necessity. At night, he often dreamed of his father, reliving the joy of working side by side, only to awaken to the cold reality of his arrest. Some nights, the dreams turned dark—his father's arrest and the look in his eyes before they were torn apart. Always sorrow, sometimes intense.

Father Kaleda's presence lingered in the hidden space. Papers and correspondence scrawled in his large, uneven handwriting remained as he had left them. Documents and a book lay scattered on the floor, marking a hurried departure. A dry teacup sat forgotten on the table, and a worn sweater hung limply by the door. For a time, Yuri left these remnants untouched, a quiet shrine to the memory of a man he had known so little, yet had come to deeply respect.

The silent evenings were the hardest, a quiet battle against an aching loneliness so deep it nearly brought him to tears. In those hours of weakness, he turned to Alyosha's example, imitating his prayers and finding peace that he was not alone. He adopted Alyosha's habits, committing long passages of Scripture to memory—a discipline that shielded his heart against despair and prepared him for an unknown future. Yet whenever he allowed himself a break from these exhausting practices, his fears returned: his status as a refugee, the crime of producing samizdat, forged travel permits, and most of all, the looming consequences of his assault on Sergei.

After a long day of work, Yuri gazed out the window, working on memorizing a passage of Scripture. Thor proudly marched by, one ear flipped inside out, oblivious to his appearance. Yuri watched as Thor approached a dripping hydrant, his ear still askew. He had seen this scene unfold before and knew exactly what was coming. The hydrant's spout was unusually high, forcing Thor to lift his head to lap at the dripping water. As always, water trickled into the back of his snout, causing him to sneeze. As expected, Thor sneezed—eight times in quick succession—his head shaking so violently that his ear flopped back into place.

Yuri's thoughts often strayed to Sabrina. The daughter of a high-ranking communist official, she was entirely out of reach, yet her memory refused to fade. He frequently replayed their brief conversation outside her home and the expression on her face the day of his arrest. Although he had removed the garments of communism, he imagined she still wore them. Even if all the barriers—her father's authority, her loyalty to the Party—could somehow be overcome, the idea that she might show interest in a penniless fugitive, or worse, a suspected assailant, seemed inconceivable.

Yuri immersed himself in his work, his days settling into a steady rhythm. Fall turned into winter. As his skill with the equipment improved, so did his output of documents. Yet, no matter how hard he labored or how much he tried to suppress it, his thoughts would drift, drawn toward an impossible hope. With no access to the conventional mail system, he began to scheme, wondering if he could somehow leverage the underground samizdat network for personal purposes. The network was tightly controlled; he had no say in where the documents ultimately ended up. Still, he took a long-shot chance, appealing to the network's courier for permission to deliver a letter to a trusted source—Ivana's parents.

Yuri lost hope. Weeks passed before permission was granted. One day, a letter arrived. The courier apologized for the delay, explaining that any new destination required thorough vetting within the underground network. Once the new route was approved, Yuri sent his first letter to Ivana's parents.

> Dear Mr. and Mrs. Beneš,
>
> Greetings, this is Yuri Dvořák. I hope you and your family are well. I'm sorry if I've put you in danger by sending you this letter or any other request. You may disregard my request if you think your family is endangered in any way. I'm sorry, I cannot tell you more about my situation.
>
> I've enclosed a letter to Sabrina Sokol. ČSM meetings are held every other week at the Lisen Cultural Center, and

she is always present. You once spoke to
me of your friend Vladimír Novák, who
attends the meetings merely for employment
opportunities and who is not sympathetic
to communism, or so I understand.

This may pose a risk for you and
Vladimír, in which case I expect you both
to prioritize your safety and disregard my
request. However, if that is not the case,
please have him pass this letter on to
Sabrina. Thank you.

Please say hello to Ivana for me. I
miss her.

Best regards,

Yuri

He enclosed the letter to Sabrina.

Dear Sabrina,

I'm sorry that I cannot write
anything about myself. The fact that
you're receiving this letter should be
enough to tell you that I'm no longer
in prison. Sometimes, I think about our
conversation when we walked together
on Šimáčkova Street. At the end of our
conversation, you didn't respond because
my words upset you, and you went home.
Have you thought more about what was said
since then?

I don't expect a response if it
endangers you in any way. Or if you're
still upset.

Srdečně,

Yuri Dvořák

His letter took flight, carrying the weight of his hopes. He chuckled at his folly for having any hope at all. Yet, each day, against hope, Yuri found himself eagerly checking for any sign of a reply.

CRISIS

LATE WINTER, 1973

Three weeks after he had posted the letter on the underground network, Zofia came for a visit. Yuri's joy at seeing her quickly turned to deep concern when he noticed her expression. Without a word, she handed him a newspaper. The headline read: "Yuri Dvořák, Son of Strike Organizer, in Hiding After Assault."

He stared at the words, his face revealing no emotion, yet inside, he felt the ground shift beneath his feet.

"Why has it taken so long for this to come out?" Yuri asked, his voice low and steady. "I mean, I kept hoping it would all be forgotten."

"Do you remember what we discussed?" Zofia replied softly, her voice low and trembling as she tried to match his calm demeanor. "Sergei risks arrest if what he did to me is revealed. He seemed to stall before making his move, but ultimately chose to take the risk. So why gamble with his reputation now? What does he hope to gain from your arrest?"

Yuri's voice turned cold. "He wants me arrested. He wants you. I'm the one standing between you and him. He took the risk. He has the money. If things turn against him, he can always flee to Vienna. He can escape; I can't."

Zofia fumed, her face flushed with anger. "Never! To the devil with him. I'll never return to him." She stood abruptly, banged the kettle on the stove, and slammed the wood box shut with a thud that echoed in the sparse, bare cottage. They both stared through the wood stove grate as the flames consumed the wood.

Yuri stood, removed the kettle from the stove, and kept Zofia's hand from adding more fuel to the fire. "You shouldn't come here anymore," he said, his voice nearly choking. "You probably shouldn't have come today. Now that you have residency in Třeboň, the secret police know where you live. They'll watch where you go, they'll . . ." He stopped, slapping his head with his palms.

"You need to leave. Now. Erase any trace of me at your home— bus tickets, documents you've taken from here, anything. Make sure Petra knows. And tell the Krčméry family too. You'll be watched— maybe worse." His voice became more constricted, "Pray that they don't take you away for interrogation; I can't imagine. . . . You can never come here again!"

Zofia stared at him, shaking her head in disbelief as the color drained from her face. "No, no."

"I need to turn myself in," Yuri said. "As long as I remain in hiding, they'll go after you. I can't bear the thought of what they'll do to you to get to me. They mustn't touch you. Either I remain in hiding and endanger you, or I turn myself in. In any case, I'm out of his way.

You still can refuse his advances. You must. I can't help you."

"Yuri, no, you can't turn yourself in!" Zofia exclaimed, becoming shrill, her anxiety choking her voice.

Yuri rose and calmly embraced his sister, holding her tightly before pulling back to gaze into her eyes for a long moment. Tears welled in both of their eyes as they silently confronted the unspoken truth—they might never see each other again.

"Be brave. Be strong. Pray," Yuri whispered. "Remember the Lord. You must go now. You need to take Thor."

Thor was tethered with the same rope Yuri had used months earlier when he said goodbye to his dog. This farewell was no less difficult. "Thor, follow," he commanded gently. Yuri stood motionless as Zofia hurried down the overgrown trail, straining at the leash of a reluctant dog, turning every few steps to steal one last glance at her brother.

Zofia waited at the bus stop, weeping. The bus arrived, the door swung open, and Thor leaped inside. "There's my old dog," the bus driver said with a smile. However, when Zofia stepped in after him, his tone cooled, and his eyes lost their friendliness. "I missed him," he said.

Only after she returned to the Krčméry's apartment, found her room, and collapsed face-down on her bed did she finally surrender to a flood of sorrow.

Yuri prepared for his departure the next morning, refusing to let his mind wander beyond the next hour for fear that despair might unravel and overwhelm him. His priority was to notify the network that the operation was shutting down. Methodically, he set about erasing all traces of life from the cottage. His belongings were packed for travel, including a few provisions: dense rye bread wrapped in paper, hard cheese, roasted chestnuts, and a few apples from the cellar.

He carefully planned his next steps. With little money, he intended to board a one-way train to Brno. If questioned about a travel pass, he would tell the truth: he was surrendering to authorities, and they could do with him as they wished.

Out of habit, he checked one last time for a response to his letter to Sabrina, expecting nothing. Absently, he opened and shut the mailbox in haste, as if to shut out yet another disappointment. An image of what he had seen was imprinted in his mind's eye—a letter had arrived! He quickly reopened the mailbox, retrieved it, and returned to the cottage, his heart pounding.

Dear Yuri,

I can hardly believe you wrote to me! I've been so worried about you since your arrest. Of course, I remember our conversation that day—how could I forget? You asked me if I was happy, and I walked away in tears. I guess that was your answer. There's so much more I want to say, but right now, something else fills my mind.

I want you to know that I pleaded with my father for weeks after your arrest. He eventually acted on your behalf to secure your release from jail. I thought I'd see you again at the ČSM meetings, just like before. My father assured me you were released, but I doubted him until Josef confirmed you were out.

Did you know you made headlines? My father hears things, and he knows about Zofia and Sergei. Yes, I know she's your sister. He even suspects why you broke in and attacked him. Yuri, I admire the courage it took to rescue her. However, my father says that what you did is very serious, and he's warned me that Zofia may also be in danger.

I remember something you told me I cannot forget: "I don't think I could live where there is no mercy." My father told me that if you returned to Brno and took the loyalty oath at the next ČSM meeting, he would do what he could to ensure you wouldn't be arrested again. He has no idea about our letters; he merely mentioned all this. I felt so proud of him when he said that—sometimes I think I see his kindness

more clearly, that he truly wants what's
best for you.

  I've enclosed a travel pass. You will
need to enter the "place of origin" since
I have no idea where you are.

  I hope you choose to return to Brno.
Oh, please come, Yuri. I can't imagine
what might happen if you don't.

  Affectionately,

  Sabrina

Yuri found himself torn between joy and grief—the sweetness of her thoughts about him, yet sorrowful for what her words implied. He hung his head, smiling grimly. *So, he acted on my behalf. . . . He has a kind heart. And that's it, then? I'm exonerated if I simply take the loyalty oath?*

Now was the time to think and plan. The timing of Sabrina's letter astounded him—it changed everything. He would have missed it had her letter been delayed by even a day. He felt relief from the urgency of his previous, almost suicidal plans. With a travel pass in hand, he decided to time his departure to coincide with the ČSM meeting. *I must attend it, but what should I do?* He planned to leave on the first Saturday in February, a day when new members were typically inducted.

With his departure now delayed, Yuri decided to write one final letter to Sabrina through the network. Whatever happened or whatever he ultimately chose, he needed to speak to her at least one more time. He ran his hand through his hair and beard, nine months of growth. *Now, I'm even starting to resemble Father Kaleda.*

The morning of February 3rd arrived quickly. The samizdat operation was mothballed. Yuri finished packing by lamplight before heading to the bus stop. He penned a letter for the next *samizdatnik*—if one could be found to carry on. He then created another envelope containing maps and instructions, similar to the one originally given to him by Father Kaleda, and kept it hidden in his overcoat. He dug to the bottom of his duffel bag and found the envelope containing details about the loyalty oath, just to make sure.

The rays of the rising sun pierced through the trees sheltering the cottage, casting fingers of light across its walls. A soft, chilly breeze stirred the air, sending a few hold-out leaves drifting lazily to the ground.

Before leaving, he paused to study the cottage, as one might linger in farewell to an old friend. The sunlight, in animated fashion, drew attention to the craftsmanship. He reached out and touched the ornate iron door knocker, his fingers tracing the floral patterns etched into the ironwork hinges. It felt as though, in touching the craftsman's work, he connected with the humanity of the long-departed artisan. He tapped the envelope beneath his coat, hoping Father Kaleda was still alive.

RENDEZVOUS

LATE WINTER, 1973

The diesel locomotive plunged toward the sunrise, propelling Yuri headlong into the unknown. He stole glances at fellow travelers, hoping none would recognize him from the newspaper photographs. He hoped his shapeless tangle of facial hair would conceal him. He gazed out the window, aware of his scruffy appearance and yearning for a life like that of the well-dressed, happy family seated nearby. He peeled chestnuts he had stuffed into his pockets and ate them; the happy family ate sandwiches.

He looked down at his hands, once callused and stained with grime, and reflected on the remarkable events of recent months: from working on tractors to enduring prison, to publishing forbidden books and manuscripts. Once again, an invisible hand seemed to guide him to places he did not wish to go. Becoming a castaway once more, his life had not grown easier, yet it felt strangely more bearable. He prayerfully considered the choices that lay before him.

I'm sad the samizdat operation shut down. If I stayed, I would have been hunted and arrested—perhaps my sisters taken hostage.

What about Sokol's pardon if I take the loyalty oath? What would I gain? My job at Zetor, the safety of my sisters, and perhaps even a girlfriend. I could find an apartment that allows dogs. Sokol might even release Táta *from jail. And what would it cost? My humanity, my soul. Once, this decision would have been simple. We survived by pretending. But I can't live that way anymore.*

What about Sokol's motives? What does he gain if I take the oath? I've promised him nothing, and he owes me nothing. I'm suspicious; I haven't thought about this enough.

Running and hiding isn't an option. My sisters would become victims. I have two options: take the oath or surrender to the secret police.

Then, another idea crossed his mind, sending a shudder through him. He ate another chestnut and fell asleep, lulled by the rhythmic, soothing sounds and vibrations of the train.

The rhythmic clatter of the train wheels slowed one final time. Yuri awoke to the sight of blocky, utilitarian apartment buildings from the communist era, interspersed with old architecture dating back to the Austro-Hungarian Empire. He transferred to the tram, which took him to the familiar Kotlanova tram stop. Finding a park bench in the ravine near his old *byt*, he huddled against the cold and waited. His food was gone, and he felt hungry.

Ivana spotted him first and broke into a run. "I saw you walking down the steps. I told my father it was you, but he didn't believe me," she giggled with delight.

"Good timing," Yuri said with a smile. "I don't blame him—I'm probably not so easy to recognize now."

She scrunched up her nose and narrowed her eyes playfully. "Yeah, you look scary, but I'm used to it." She extended her hand as a gesture of reconciliation.

Standing, Yuri took her little hand with three of his fingers, bowed respectfully, and gently kissed it. "You're not afraid of me? I'm stunned by your kindness," he said, humoring her further.

"How is Zofia?" she inquired.

He sighed deeply, nodding and shrugging before he said, "She's doing just fine."

"Are you sure?" she started to ask, but her father interrupted her.

"Hello, Yuri," Mr. Beneš greeted. "I almost didn't recognize you."

"I know, tell me about it," Yuri replied with a polite smile. "Thank you for coming and taking the risk." He subtly checked for the envelope in his pocket.

Yuri spoke cautiously while recounting the last few months, not out of distrust for Mr. Beneš, but for his safety. This way, if ever questioned, Mr. Beneš could honestly deny any knowledge of Yuri's activities. He explained to Mr. Beneš that he would be cleared of all offenses against the State in exchange for taking part in the upcoming loyalty-oath ceremony.

Ivana wandered off to explore, and Yuri seized the moment. "Before you go, I have something for you," he said, handing Mr. Beneš a prepared envelope concealed within a folded newspaper. "Inside, you will find an envelope. Keep it well hidden. If no one asks for it after six months, burn it. I can't tell you what's inside, but as I mentioned, the *Státní bezpečnost* must never find this. However, if someone approaches you and says, 'Yuri says you have an envelope for me,' then hand it over to that person. That's all. Most likely, nothing will come of it."

After they parted ways, Ivana left her father's side and returned to Yuri. "You look hungry," she said, offering him a stale holiday bear paw cookie wrapped in wax paper. He devoured it the moment she was out of sight.

Yuri first heard the rapid staccato of her footsteps as Sabrina descended the stairs from the tram stop. Looking up, their eyes met, and her pace slowed. Yuri adjusted his appearance, erasing the powdery evidence of a bear paw from his beard and mustache. *She always sees me when I look my worst.*

He stood, and for a moment, they faced each other. She looked perfect and unapproachable, as always, he mused. He felt the tension as she lingered briefly, her eyes studying him. Words failed him. She seemed to look past his rough exterior to the man he had become—his face conveyed a dignity shaped by hardship. Though clouded with embarrassment, his eyes held a concealed joy and strength. His unease melted away when she unexpectedly drew him into a gentle embrace.

They sat together on a bench chiseled from a wooden log, both too self-conscious to break the silence. *I never thought of Sabrina as a quiet one,* he thought, recalling her confidently leading a ČSM meeting. He peeled a sliver from the bench and flicked it away.

"It's very nice to see you. I see you got my message," Yuri said calmly.

"It's nice to see you, too. You're clever with your mode of communication," Sabrina replied, suppressing a thousand questions.

"I'm sorry I couldn't make myself more presentable today . . ."

"It's nothing. Don't even think about it," she replied briskly, yet nervously.

After a pause, Yuri asked, "You're probably going to urge me to swear the loyalty oath at tonight's meeting, aren't you?"

Sabrina hesitated. He looked at her, surprised by her silence. She wrapped her wool coat more snugly around herself and tightened her belt.

"What? Tell me," he inquired.

"My father's offer to pardon you in exchange for pledging the oath isn't quite what you think. He will still pardon you, but there's a catch."

She paused, glancing at Yuri to gauge his reaction. He remained unmoved, his lips slightly pursed. Gradually, he met her gaze, his eyes smiling as if to say, "Of course. As you were saying?"

". . . Well, Josef told me. He overheard his father speaking with mine. Sergei—the same guy in the newspaper, you know who I mean—he's paying off my father to have you exonerated. Your loyalty oath is just a way for my father to save face. The real catch is that your freedom is conditioned on your not interfering with your sister's relationship with Sergei and her not rejecting him."

Yuri remembered to breathe, shook his head, and muttered, "So, that's how it's going to be. If I were arrested, Zofia would hate Sergei forever. However, she would feel indebted to him if he arranged for my freedom, as would I, or so he thinks."

She paused. "You're still going to take the oath, yes?" When he didn't answer, she asked more urgently, "Well, aren't you?"

Yuri replied, "I am surprised you responded to my letter and met me today. Such a meeting seems impossible, given my situation. My recent living circumstances have left me . . . not quite myself when I wrote."

"You make me feel sad every time we talk," she said, yet she didn't walk away.

Encouraged that she felt anything, Yuri continued, "I see many reasons why you should avoid me. Your family's status provides you with educational and career opportunities. Even if I were absolved by taking the oath, I would always be a factory worker. Maybe I'm assuming too much, but my status would only hold you back. And do you think your father would approve of you associating with someone who has a soiled reputation? So much for a classless society. And he wouldn't want me around as a reminder of the deal he made with Sergei."

Trying to lighten the mood, he added with a smile, "Besides, I still talk like a *vidlák*. . . . Tell me, how are those handsome guys who played so well on the *fotbol* team? Tomáš, Luboš, Radek. . . ."

"Shut up. You're not going to take the oath, are you? You know what will happen," she said, leaning forward and grasping her knees with her arms.

Yuri expressed profound sorrow.

"Do you care about what I do? There's no future for me."

"Where have you been all these months? What have you been doing?" she inquired.

Yuri didn't answer her initial question. He cautiously explained his work in producing samizdat. He understood he was taking a serious risk, particularly since the network courier was indirectly associated with Sabrina.

As he recounted details of the banned literature he reproduced—the Bible and other forbidden texts—he studied her expression intently, gauging how much he could reveal. He couldn't conceal the delight he felt in describing his work.

"You see, nearly every day since my release from prison, I've been breaking the law. It was an amazing experience."

"Oh, be quiet. Why are you telling me this? Why do you speak about it that way?" she said.

Yuri held back from replying, *Because you asked.* He knew Sabrina understood the risk he was taking by testing her trust with such confidential information.

This was not the direction she had hoped their conversation would take.

"Given your role in the ČSM and your family connections, I probably shouldn't be talking to you. And yet, here you are. I'm sharing these thoughts for many reasons, but mainly because I hope that who you are on the inside is different from who you're pretending to be."

Sabrina stood up, ready to defend herself against this affront, but held back, not finding the words.

"I only wish for you to become as I am—to have joy and freedom of conscience, yet without my troubles."

After a brief pause, she sat again and wrapped her hands around his arm, gently holding it against her, securing the fleeting moments.

"I don't have much time," she murmured. "I just want you to talk to me. Tell me about your life."

The sincerity of the gesture caught Yuri off guard. After months of crushing loneliness, he fought back a wave of emotion, struggling to find his voice.

When he steadied his breathing, he began to share the sad story of his parents—his mother's death, his father's unusual grief and determination to strike at Zetor, his mother's grave, his own regrets, his sister and Sergei, and the Scripture verse that changed his life.

He spoke more about his sisters, the love and respect he held for his father, and the months he spent working in a deep basement, enduring hardships and learning tough but rewarding lessons.

Sabrina listened, then quietly replied, "I loved my father as a child. He meant everything to me. As I grew older, I began to hear things I didn't want to believe. I noticed his dark moods and his anger. I felt ashamed around my friends because of the smell of alcohol and cigarette smoke. I struggled to see the good in him. I needed, I wanted to be proud of him. I was overjoyed when he released you from prison, and I heard he'd offered to pardon you. You can't imagine how happy I was. And then . . . the disappointment of what I learned from Josef."

She paused. "You think my life is so great. You have no idea how fortunate you are to have a father you respect—even if he's now just a memory."

This turn in the conversation was unexpected. They stood and faced each other, nearly eye to eye. Their expressions showed that they both understood the contrast between them—material wealth and future security on one side, poverty and uncertainty on the other—yet also the difference between dissatisfaction with life and settled contentment. Yuri looked long at Sabrina, she could not hold his gaze. Their conversation was coming to a close. He slowly shook his head.

Then an idea came to him. He took her cold hands in his.

"You probably know how tonight will turn out. I'll tell you

what I told my sister: 'Be brave. Be strong.' Don't endanger yourself needlessly. I won't think less of you, whatever you do. Go on with life and forget about me. Really. But if anything I've said rings true, if you're ready to resist Communism and carry on the work I'm leaving behind with the underground church . . ."

He gave her directions to the Beneš family. "Simply tell them, 'Yuri sent me to collect an envelope.' You have six months to consider it. They will hold onto it for that long before destroying it."

Sabrina listened, imagining what this life would mean—and what she would be leaving behind.

She exhaled slowly. "I don't know," she said. "Why?"

She looked down at their clasped hands, then softly pulled away.

"As I said before, you always make me feel sad every time we speak. Goodbye, Yuri."

She turned and walked away. Yuri pondered the sudden change in mood, questioning whether he had upset her. She stopped, returned to him, gently kissed his cheek, and departed again quickly. He fought back tears as he watched her run up the steps out of the ravine.

She managed to hold back her tears until she was seated on the tram.

LOYALTY OATH

LATE WINTER, 1973

Yuri stood at the end of the line of ČSM applicants, ready to take the loyalty oath. He wondered why he had been placed last and wished the ordeal would end soon. Those without notes radiated with confidence, having memorized the oath to display their loyalty. Though Yuri also held no notes, he trembled at what he was about to say.

The applicants recited the oath in predictable, monotonous tones, one by one, followed by warm handshakes from the ČSM leaders. The atmosphere was consistently dull; the seats creaked, and a soft undertone of whispering filled the air. Yuri looked curiously at the speakers. He peered behind him. *I've never noticed the deadness in their eyes.*

Before sitting down, each applicant received the coveted party pin, followed by polite applause. Congratulations from higher-ranking officials, emphasizing the applicants' new responsibilities and the gravity of their commitment, were reserved for the final pledge.

Yuri observed how some smiled broadly as if this membership had been a lifelong ambition. He could distinguish the true believers from those merely going through the motions, pretenders, seeking only the career or educational advantages of party membership. Their eyes told the story.

Finally, Yuri stood at the podium, gazing at the attendees, gathering his thoughts, and calming his emotions. He ran his hand through his shaggy beard. A murmur spread through the auditorium as people leaned toward one another, their eyes fixed on him. Eventually, the room fell silent. He noticed the same four men he'd seen lingering outside before his arrival. Their attempt to remain unseen only made them more conspicuous as they entered the meeting and positioned themselves mostly out of view behind the pillars.

Yuri expected to see Sokol, who had summoned him to make this public declaration of loyalty. His absence and the presence of the four men puzzled him.

Wasn't this meant for him? Wasn't Sokol the reason I was summoned to take this oath?

He shrugged it off.

"You all know who I am. I've been away for a while, but it's good to be back. I'm grateful to many of you—the memory of your friendship over the past months sustained me through . . . difficult times recently. In case you forgot, I'm Yuri Dvořák."

The auditorium fell unusually quiet as everyone recognized exactly who was speaking to them, breaking protocol from the usual monotony. The man before them resembled the Yuri they once knew, yet he appeared older, tempered by suffering but unbroken, with a smile in his eyes. He was noticeably more shaggy and poorly dressed, ill-suited for such a solemn occasion. He spoke freely and calmly, scanning their faces. Some turned away, avoiding his gaze, unwilling to reveal any connection to him. Others, convinced of the threat he posed, scowled, their expressions reflecting a mix of anger and fear. A hopeful few suspended judgment, intrigued by his honesty.

His gaze fell on Sabrina. Normally seated at the front during such events, particularly when officiating, she was now positioned near the back, her eyes wide and unblinking.

"I have fond memories of playing *fotbol* with many of you, of our debates, and the cultural festivals. . . . I often recalled those moments during my darkest hours," he said.

Yuri paused, then continued, "Now, you expect me to pledge my loyalty and allegiance to the Communist Party of Czechoslovakia and the socialist state. . . . I will not."

A murmur rippled through the room, followed by silence. The four inconspicuous men glanced at one another and then around the room as if searching for someone. The events of this night were expected to be routine.

Yuri continued, not with a combative tone but maintaining a calm, pleading sincerity. The young people listened in silence, not swayed by his eloquence but by the simple truth in his words.

"Let's stop pretending. At the entrance to this meeting, you displayed a poster: 'Youth for Peace!' Was Russia's military occupation in 1968 a gesture of 'peace'? 'Oh,' they say, 'We offered you our fraternal assistance,' and yet today, you can still see scars on our buildings from the tanks that rolled into this city.

"Another poster reads: 'Freedom for the Working Class!' Strikers at the Zetor Tractor Factory were offered freedom—the freedom to choose between returning to work or facing imprisonment at gunpoint. And then there's: 'Liberty is Born from Equality!' What liberty does my father have? He has vanished from our lives. Who knows what torture he endures now? Was the legal code fairly upheld in the interest of my liberty when I was held and tortured for three months to force a confession? I would still be in prison if not for a friend with influence.

"And here's yet another slogan: 'Forward for Socialism!' Has socialism truly moved you 'forward' when there's a limited selection of basic goods and long lines to get food or clothing? When the shop attendants say, 'Keep coming back,' do they actually mean, 'don't bother coming back'? Our family once owned a small farm. Did we advance 'forward' when this farm was confiscated from us?

"We're promised unity and brotherhood. Oh, how these words

warm our hearts. Who among us doesn't want unity and brotherhood? But these benefactors of unity have left my family fractured and broken. I've been forced into hiding, isolated and lonely, out of fear of our beloved 'unifying' Party authorities. You live in constant distrust, watching one another warily, afraid that a neighbor—or even a family member—might inform on you for something, or nothing at all.

"And what of 'freedom of thought'? We have it abundantly, as long as it conforms to socialist values. How rich our lives have become, and how enlightened by a forced diet of state-controlled education and media. But you wouldn't dare teach your children from the Bible or anything contrary to what is prescribed by the State. . . ."

Yuri watched as Sokol rushed into the room. The four inconspicuous men swiftly approached him, speaking in low voices. Sabrina had her head in her hands.

Yuri continued speaking, his gaze tracking the men as a sixth— the Bear—joined them, all moving toward him.

The auditorium seemed not to breathe. One might wonder who was the master and who the prisoner. The young people marveled at how long Yuri spoke, as if those few moments stretched into hours. As if he were in control and not those preparing to overpower him.

With a steady gaze, a calm voice, and a slight smile in his eyes, he concluded, "Remember me when I'm in prison. Walk in the truth. This regime will run out of steam if you do."

The four men moved with casual deliberation, careful not to raise alarm. They knew how precarious their position was and how easily Yuri's words and charm could turn hearts against them. They urged Yuri to follow without laying a hand on him. They escorted him out of the building under the watchful eyes of everyone present. He remembered years ago, when he was the one to carry his adversary out of the cafeteria by force.

Sabrina stood up, broke through the circle of secret police, and grabbed Yuri's arm as if to pull him back. They pushed her aside. In the hallway, she began beating upon the back of one of the police officers, her voice rising in protest. The Bear, flushed with anger at her interference and the scene she was creating, aggressively seized her arm to pull her back. She fell to the ground. He stared in disbelief at who it was—Sokol's daughter. Sabrina got up and followed them out of the building, ignoring Sokol's shout, "Sabrina, please stop!"

She observed four nondescript men force Yuri into an unmarked car, vanishing with him into the night.

RIPPLES

SUMMER INTO FALL, 1973

Zofia lay in bed, staring into the darkness before dawn, watching as the light touched the tops of the trees and then descended upon the buildings. Rising, she sat on the edge of her bed next to Petra, whispering prayers for her brother and *Táta*, her thoughts returning to the stories Yuri told of his time in prison—stories extracted from him by what he called her "witchery." She recalled moments during the day, as they worked on producing samizdat, when the past slipped through the cracks, his breath would quicken, his hands would clench, and he'd stop working to stare into space. *Yuri had his scars.*

Zofia assumed the worst: *Yuri hadn't taken the oath. He turned himself in. He was arrested again. He could be with* Táta *in prison. More torture. More scars. . . . O, Lord, for what purpose?* Her mind wandered to a memory from years earlier, when, as a girl in a new dress in the cafeteria, Yuri had defended her honor and accepted the punishment. *He ran into trouble for me then, too.*

Each day, Zofia and Petra walked to the collective newspaper kiosk, scanning the paper on their way back for news of Yuri. Nothing. For Petra, who hadn't seen Yuri since his first week in Kolence, the danger he faced felt distant and unreal. She had already concluded that he was throwing away his life. If he were now in prison, his life would have been wasted only by another degree. But the reality of his condition became painfully clear days later when they discovered a headline buried on the fifth page: *Yuri Dvořák, Fugitive, Assailant, Arrested Again*. She read it again. Then again.

"Yuri must be at Věznice na Cejlu," Zofia mused aloud. Even the sound of this infamous prison, in Brno, had a chilling effect. The sisters gathered in the kitchen with Jaroslav and Emilie Krčméry that evening. Jaroslav leaned forward, elbows on the table, worry etched into the lines on his face.

"We'll ask after him. . . But careful-like. No making a big fuss. I've already stuck my neck out, keeping you girls here—and don't think I'd take it back, I wouldn't—but we can't go kicking up dust. Let me be the one to write the request. Best if it comes from me."

Weeks passed without a response. Zofia wrote to Ivana's parents, hoping they might have some information. Once again, nothing. They concluded that all their mail to Brno had been intercepted. Even worse, they suspected the State now knew Zofia and Petra's whereabouts, and that they were being watched.

Months later, Zofia listened to the steady drumming of rain against the metal roof and bus window. The sky was ominously and delightfully dark, with distant lightning illuminating the overcast

sky. The bus driver still avoided eye contact; his previous coolness
had given way to cold looks. She arrived at Kolence, wrapped in a
borrowed raincoat, and began the long walk to Father Kaleda's cottage.
The rain and the hood of her coat provided concealment—she had
chosen a good day to travel. The cottage was unchanged since Yuri's
departure, except for a new family of mice that had taken up residence.
Thor's bowls, hastily left behind, were now filled with rainwater and
drowned earthworms. She noticed new saplings sprouting from the
mossy roof. Sitting on the doorstep, she scraped the mud from her
boots with a stick, unbothered by the fact that she would collect more
on the return trip.

Memories came like a flood—most of them happy. She offered
a prayer of thanks for the work and the time she shared with Yuri.
She complained upward: *What was the point of the strike at Zetor?
Nothing has changed—everything is worse. And the samizdat? Does
anyone read it? We are too weak; the State is too strong.* She had
come to create a tangible connection with Yuri, to relive the memories
they shared. The memories exhausted themselves; she was left feeling
sweetly miserable. The rain had stopped, a grey sky remained, and the
air grew cooler. And Zofia had an idea.

She entered the cottage and wrote a letter to the Beneš family,
requesting a clandestine meeting and asking them to bring Ivana.
Carefully, she placed it in the hidden dead drop that Yuri had often used
for communication in the underground network.

As she departed, she resolved never to come back.

On the day of the rendezvous, Zofia borrowed a bicycle and
rode through Třeboň to the Park of the Schwarzenberg Tomb. She sat
on the north-facing steps, scanning every person who emerged from
the tree-lined path into the open park area. Moments ticked by. "What
were the chances?" she whispered to herself in disbelief that her plan
worked. Ivana broke into a run, arriving before her father. Zofia and
Ivana embraced each other. Ivana had so much to tell. This rendezvous
of old friends brought pangs of joy and grief. Memories of their hours
together came flooding back.

After her father sat beside Zofia, Ivana squeezed and wriggled
in between them. They sat together in silence, making sure no one
suspicious had followed. She was eager to hear anything about Yuri.
Her suspense was delayed as Mr. Beneš mentioned the new tenants in
Zofia's old apartment: their old furniture and the remains of the balcony
garden were all discarded. Zofia listened impatiently as Mr. Beneš
spoke in praise of all the books she had transcribed, which, he said,

would become a seedbed from which Ivana would someday grow into a dissident. Ivana squirmed in hearty acknowledgement. Zofia was not interested.

"And what about Yuri? Have you heard anything?" she asked impatiently.

Alexei Beneš told her all about the conversation he had with Yuri in the park. He further shared what he had learned from Vladimír Novák about the night of Yuri's arrest. Zofia was stunned.

"Unbelievable. He never intended to submit to the loyalty oath. He did this for me. He got the last word in. He went out triumphantly. It still seems such a waste. What difference does it all make? He's gone."

Zofia could no longer withhold her tears. People visiting the park stopped and looked as Zofia abandoned herself to grief. The sun hid its face behind a cloud.

"Zofia, but it wasn't a waste, not entirely," said Mr. Beneš with gentleness.

Zofia looked up at him with red eyes and a tear-stained face.

"There's more," he continued. "Vladimír has kept his membership at the ČSM to appear loyal and to secure a better education—until recently. Most of us would do the same, yes? Pretending out of fear—that's what we always do. He's a quiet lad who keeps to himself. But Yuri's defiant speech has left an impression on him and a few others. There are small acts of resistance, like ripples. Some no longer wear party pins. Applause has grown weak, with claps half-hearted. Some have even begun wearing cross necklaces they make themselves, hidden under their shirts.

"In the past, speakers at the meeting went unchallenged. Now, they are questioned, not openly enough to break the rules, but just enough to disrupt. Propaganda posters, once dutifully displayed before every meeting, were defaced with the small symbol 'YD?' in the lower corner, a quiet homage to Yuri. Vladimír told me that the posters were later taken down, not only because of the defacement but also because of the growing resistance.

"Then there's Václav Havel, the dissident. He's been publishing essays through the underground, critiquing the regime's suppression of freedom and individuality. Vladimír showed me a copy he received. It's remarkable. These have been discreetly circulated during the ČSM meetings. The last I heard, Vladimír had stopped attending the meetings entirely, giving up whatever educational advantage he may have received. And he's not alone; others have stopped as well. This is a big deal. It's such a sacrifice."

Unbelievable, Zofia thought, hungry for every word.

Mr. Beneš continued, "Their control is slipping. These acts of resistance are like small signals, quietly passed from one soul to another. As I mentioned, they're like ripples; instead of fading, they're growing stronger. And instead of being limited, they're multiplying."

He paused before adding, "You may be interested in what is happening at Zetor since the strike. I was on the second shift and missed the fireworks on the day of the strike. Things have since changed. It's the small things, the details that slip under the radar, like work slowdowns. Workers deliberately slow their pace or operate machinery at lower speeds. They say, 'Quality comes first,' yet more tractors are failing quality control. There's underground literature circulating as well—poetry, essays, and even cartoons mocking the party authorities. I could go on."

Zofia sat in silence, pondering what she had just heard. After a moment, she glanced up at Mr. Beneš, "This is all . . . amazing. Yuri made the sacrifice for me. Yet, he and *Táta* started something so much more. But the cost is more than I can bear."

Mr. Beneš glanced toward the tree line, where a family was collecting mushrooms. "That reminds me—about two weeks ago, after our family returned from gathering mushrooms in the Líšeň Woods, a young woman came to our door. We had never met her, and she didn't introduce herself, but she was polite and well-dressed. She's obviously not from our neighborhood, if you know what I mean. Oh, and she was quite tall. She said, 'You don't know me, but you might understand what I'm about to say. Yuri sent me to pick up an envelope. Can you help me with this?'"

Zofia stared into the distance, her heartbeat quickening as a faint smile touched her lips. "Trust me, it's good news," she replied softly. Then, glancing at Mr. Beneš with a resigned expression and a shrug, she added, "But that's all I can tell you. I'm sorry."

Zofia returned to Kaleda's cottage after all. Thor followed her. As she gathered a few chanterelle mushrooms along the path, the scent of wood smoke drifted through the trees. She paused. Thor paused and growled low, his snout pointing into the air. When the cottage came into view, she saw smoke rising from the flue pipe. Someone was there. Her steps became more resolute, but then she slowed her pace. This person was a friend of Yuri's, yes, but she didn't know who it might be, not with certainty.

Pausing in sight of the cottage, she called out with her contralto voice, "Hello?" She moved closer, assuming her appearance would disarm the occupant. Thor became more relaxed and marched up to inspect his water and supper bowls.

"Hello?" Zofia cried out again. She remembered that Sabrina had only met her a couple of times. Thor put his front paws on the doorstep and barked once. The heavy cottage door opened slowly, and a tall brunette stood in its frame, hesitant to go further. Thor backed away, put his head down, and growled.

"Sabrina?" Zofia questioned. "Is it you? Do you remember me? I'm Zofia. Yuri's brother." And then, as though to disarm Sabrina's apprehension and give herself an excuse for making the trip, she said, "I've brought you some chanterelles."

Sabrina left the cottage and cautiously approached Zofia. "Of course, I remember you. Thank you for coming. We have so much to talk about." Ignoring the outstretched bag of chanterelles, Sabrina embraced her new friend.

"Please stay for tea," Sabrina asked.

"I, I am he who comforts you;
who are you that you are afraid of man who dies,
of the son of man who is made like grass,
and have forgotten the Lord, your Maker,
who stretched out the heavens
and laid the foundations of the earth,
and you fear continually all the day
because of the wrath of the oppressor,
when he sets himself to destroy?
And where is the wrath of the oppressor?
He who is bowed down shall speedily be released;
he shall not die and go down to the pit,
neither shall his bread be lacking."
— Isaiah 51:12-14 ESV

"For what does it profit a man to gain the
whole world and forfeit his soul?"
— Mark 8:36 ESV

Appendix I: Key Characters

Dvořák Family

Jana Dvořák — Yuri, Zofia, and Petra's mother. Wife of Václav.

Petra Dvořáková – The youngest sibling, optimistic and warm-hearted, yet quick to anger. She embodies the ideal Communist woman and balances Zofia's seriousness.

Václav Dvořák – Yuri, Zofia, and Petra's father, a former military officer and a significant figure in the workers' movement.

Yuri Dvořák – The main protagonist.

Zofia Dvořáková – The youngest sibling, introverted, scholarly. Independent and reserved, she is deeply introspective.

Allies and Resistance Figures

Alexei Beneš – Ivana's father, a factory worker at Zetor who secretly sympathizes with the resistance.

Alyosha – Yuri's friend and fellow prisoner, known for his unwavering faith and optimism despite harsh conditions.

Emilie Krčméry – Jaroslav's wife.

Father Kaleda – A Husite priest who provides spiritual and moral guidance to Yuri.

Ivana Benešová – A young girl fascinated by books and storytelling. She deeply admires Zofia.

Jaroslav Krčméry – A trusted ally of Václav Dvořák. He provides shelter and guidance to Zofia and Petra after their father's arrest.

Miloslav — A dedicated factory worker and a close ally of Václav Dvořák in organizing the strike at the Zetor Tractor Factory.

Sabrina Sokol – The daughter of a high-ranking Communist Party official, Svoboda Sokol. Her character arc is closely tied to Yuri.

Opponents and Antagonists

Josef – A member of the ČSM and an antagonist to Yuri. Josef is initially confrontational but later reveals a more complex nature.

Sergei – Fatal love interest for Zofia.

Svoboda Sokol – A high-ranking party official who attempts to recruit Yuri into the Communist Party.

The Bear (Josef's Father) — A brutal and imposing figure, Josef's father is a member of the secret police.

Vlasta — known as "the Man-Slayer" is a ruthless interrogator who uses psychological manipulation, seduction, and violence to extract confessions from prisoners.

Appendix II: Czech Terminology and Cultural References

Agriculture Commissar — A government-appointed official enforcing production quotas on collective farms.

Battle of Sokolovo (March 1943) — A Czechoslovak-Soviet engagement against Nazi forces, referenced in Václav's military background.

Bulgakov, Mikhail, *Master and Margarita* — A banned novel satirizing Stalinism circulated illegally as samizdat.

Brontë, Charlotte, *Jane Eyre*, ed. Margaret Smith (Oxford: Oxford University Press, 2000), 436. The original line reads: "Nature had surely formed her in a partial mood; and, forgetting her usual stinted step-mother dole of gifts, had endowed this, her darling, with a grand-dame's bounty."

Byt — *Apartment*. An apartment or dwelling in an urban residential complex.

Bytové dílny — *Apartment workshops*. Private homes used by dissidents to print and distribute banned literature during the communist era.

Československé státní dráhy — *Czechoslovak State Railways*. The national railway company, highly regulated under communist rule, with travel permits required for long-distance journeys.

Československý Svaz Mládeže (ČSM) — *The Czechoslovak Union of Youth*. A state-sponsored youth organization used for ideological indoctrination.

Česnečka — *Czech garlic soup*. Traditional soup often used to remedy colds or warm up during harsh winters.

Chambers, Whittaker (1901–1961) – An American writer and former Soviet spy who defected from Communism and became a vocal anti-Communist. In his memoir *Witness* (1952), Chambers reflects on the moral and spiritual crises that drive individuals toward Communism, stating, "The crisis makes men Communists, and the crisis keeps them

Communists."

Dobré ráno — *Good morning.*

Fotbal — *Soccer.* A popular sport throughout Czechoslovakia.

Forced Collectivization — The state takeover of private farms after 1948, leading to mass displacement and persecution of resisting farmers.

Havel, Václav (1936 - 2011) — A dissident playwright whose essays critiqued the regime and influenced the resistance leading to the Velvet Revolution.

Homer, *The Odyssey*, trans. Robert Fagles (New York: Viking Penguin, 1996), Book 11, lines 180–185. — Inspiration for the line *"He was wasting away the nights, weeping away the days."*

Hus, Jan (1369–1415) — A Czech reformer and martyr, invoked as a symbol of standing against tyranny.

Kafka, Franz, *The Metamorphosis* – A Czech writer whose novella tells the story of Gregor Samsa, a man who inexplicably transforms into a giant insect.

Kolchozní byty — *Collective farm apartments.* Drab, utilitarian housing for workers on state-run collective farms.

Maminka— *Mom,* or *Mommy.*

Ministry of the Interior — Oversaw law enforcement, surveillance, and suppression of dissent.

Na shledanou — *Goodbye* or *See you later.*

New Faith — A term describing the Marxist-Leninist ideology, promoted as a replacement for traditional religious beliefs by Communist regimes.

Paneláky — *Panel buildings.* Built under Communist rule, they reflect the gray uniformity of everyday life for many characters.

Předseda — *Chairman* or *leader*. Director or chairman of a state-run collective enterprise.

Slečna — *Miss*. A young woman.

Státní bezpečnost — *State security*. Czechoslovak secret police.

StB — *Secret Police*. Operated as an arm of state repression, monitoring and interrogating dissidents.

Straníci — *Party members*. Communist Party officials overseeing farms and industries, ensuring ideological conformity.

Táta / Tatko — *Dad* or *Daddy*.

Tolkien, J.R.R., *The Fellowship of the Ring* (Boston: Houghton Mifflin, 1994), 290. The quote "Faithless is he that says farewell when the road darkens" is spoken by Gimli in Lothlórien, affirming his loyalty to the Fellowship in the face of danger.

Večeře — *Evening meal*. Traditionally hearty and simple, often featuring bread, cheese, potatoes, and soups.

Věznice na Cejlu — *Cejl prison in Brno*. A notorious Brno prison used to hold political prisoners during the Communist era, often associated with StB interrogations.

Vidlák — *Pitchfork person*. A derogatory term meaning "country bumpkin" or "rustic."

Acknowledgments

I owe a debt of gratitude to *Live Not By Lies* by Rod Dreher. I learned how many people in Eastern Europe lived fearlessly under totalitarianism, how their resistance eventually broke the back of ideological imprisonment, and how the same courage is relevant in today's culture. This is also how I want to live. I'm also grateful for a few friends who so kindly read this book and offered their suggestions, among whom are Jim Elliff, my wife, Jane, Daniel Pentimone, and Claire Snell.